KASTHURI GRADUATES

HITAPRADA

ISBN
Paperback 979-8-89906-285-8
Hardcase 979-8-89961-802-4

Dedication

To the cherished memory of my beloved grandmother, who was loved by all of us as 'Avva'.

Miss You

Heartfelt Gratitude

To Dr. N. Chandrasekhara, for his invaluable guidance and unwavering support.

To my beloved husband, Seshu, my most honest critic and greatest supporter.

To my darling daughter Bindu, my constant cheerleader and a source of strength.

To my dear brother Sagar, for believing in this book more than I did.

Chapter 1

It was the monsoon month of August 1920. Rain had been pouring incessantly since the previous night in the picturesque, charming hill town of Sakleshpur, nestled amidst beautiful mountains and deep valleys, renowned for its vast coffee and pepper plantations. Though it was 6:00 am, the Sun was in no mood to appear from behind the dark clouds. Occasional thunder, lightning, a whistling breeze, and big fat drops of continuous downpour made one doubt whether the rain would stop anytime soon.

Keshavamurthy had just finished his bath and looked out from the verandah at the lashing downpour while wiping his head with a cotton towel. Keshavamurthy Iyengar, popularly known as Coffee *Thote* Keshavamurthy among the town dwellers, was a tall, wheatish-complexioned, well-built man. He owned a sprawling coffee estate that grew both Robusta and Arabica varieties, and was wealthy and affluent.

"Hope the rains don't affect the yield this year," he muttered as he walked into the house towards the puja room. "Alamelu! I am starting with the puja. Is the *Naivedya* ready?" he asked his wife.

"Yes, yes, *Sakre Pongal* is almost ready," Alamelamma answered from the kitchen. Alamelamma, Keshavamurthy's wife, was a short, plump, fair-complexioned lady and a great homemaker. By then, she had also bathed and looked graceful in a bright navy blue 9-yard sari with an equally bright pink border draped in the traditional *madisaa*r style. She tied her thick, jet-black hair into a tight bun, and a bright red vermilion *bindi* adorned her broad forehead.

Like every morning, Alamelamma was busy in the kitchen. She was frying cashews and raisins in a bit of ghee to add to the day's *naivedyam* and preparing *Chitranna* for the younger children to take to school. She then filled the large brass coffee percolator with hot water and six large spoonfuls of freshly ground coffee powder to make a strong decoction to meet the family's coffee needs for the day. The appetising smell of food and the pleasant aroma of brewing coffee wafted from the kitchen and filled the entire house.

As Keshavamurthy sat in the puja room, clearing the flowers and garlands from the previous day, he suddenly remembered that the plumber was arriving at the estate early that morning to repair a few clogged plumbing lines. "I should remind Narayana to open the estate gates early today," he thought. "Alamelu, has Narayana woken up? Could you ask him to go to the estate and open the gates for the plumber?"

"Yes. I will!" Alamelu answered from the kitchen.

The couple's eldest son, Narayana, the first among Keshavamurthy's five children, was 16. He was a physical replica of his father: tall, well-built, and good-looking. Although Keshavamurthy enrolled his older son in the nearby Mission School, attending school and learning never appealed to Narayana, and he dropped out after a few months, much to his father's disappointment.

"Narayana, good education not only makes a person wiser and more confident but also makes one self-reliant." Keshavamurthy would try to reason. However, Narayana would turn a deaf ear to his father's advice and instead preferred to while away his time wandering around the town with his equally non-enterprising friends. He was a cause of constant worry for his parents.

"You are not allowed to while away your time in useless chatter with your friends. You either attend school or come with me to the estate every day. I need a helping hand at the estate." Keshavamurthy issued an ultimatum.

Given no choice, Narayana reluctantly went to the estate with his father every morning. However, he showed no interest in the estate's affairs. He would laze around and secretly steal a puff when his father wasn't looking. Keshavamurthy, however, hoped that he would eventually learn to manage the estate.

By now, Keshavamurthy had cleared the previous day's flowers and cleaned the puja room. He turned to look back at the jingling sound of anklets. It was Pankaja, his older daughter. "*Appa,* here are the garlands for the deities," Pankaja handed over the beautifully twined multi-coloured garlands to her father.

"The garlands look all the more beautiful today, Jalaja. You and your sister are becoming experts in making garlands by the day", Keshavamurthy remarked appreciatively.

"*Appa*! I'm Pankaja! You always get confused."

"Sorry, *Kannamma*! You and your sister are exact replicas of each other. Even your mother gets confused at times. You cannot blame me. Can you?" Keshavamurthy laughingly teased his older daughter.

The couple's second and third children were identical twin daughters, Pankaja and Jalaja, who were 14 years old. They were both lean and pretty-looking girls. They dressed identically in similar sarees and were quite close to each other. They enjoyed each other's company and would often chat and laugh away.

Although girls attending schools and colleges was unheard of during those days, Keshavamurthy Iyengar firmly believed in girls' right to education and enrolled both girls at the nearby Hardwicke Mission school.

"*Appa,* we are the only girls in a class full of boys. Also, most of our teachers are male. We feel extremely uncomfortable in school. We prefer to stay home and practice our music," Pankaja said, while Jalaja nodded in agreement.

"My darlings! Haven't you heard of Kadambini Ganguly, the first woman to graduate from India? She was the only girl in her class and in her entire school. However, she didn't give up. Did she?" Keshavamurthy would try to inspire his daughters to pursue their studies.

"Why do you bother the girls? We would have to get them married soon anyway. They would rather learn to cook and practice their music," Alamelamma would intervene, as she had always been averse to sending her daughters to school. Due to their mother's strong support, the girls refused to attend school, and Keshavamurthy had no say.

Pankaja played the *Veena* well, while Jalaja was a trained Carnatic classical singer. The twin sisters enjoyed gardening and nurtured various flowering plants in their front yard while also helping their mother with household chores.

Early marriages were the norm in those days, and at his wife's behest, Keshavamurthy Iyengar searched for suitable alliances for his two older daughters.

By now, Keshavamurthy was immersed in chanting holy hymns and offering his prayers to the deities when Kasthuri's voice rang through the house, disturbing the calm, as she chased her little brother. "Stop right there, Bhagwan! Give me back my ribbons, you little brat!" Kasthuri screamed as she ran behind Bhagwan.

The 11-year-old Kasthuri, the couple's fourth child and third daughter, was the brightest and Keshavamurthy's favourite. Keshavamurthy doted on Kasthuri and would affectionately call her *"Ammani."*

Kasthuri was a bubbly, cheerful, and beautiful girl of medium height, with a fair complexion and an endearing smile. She attended the Hardwicke Mission School with her 9-year-old brother, Bhagwan. Her passion for learning was strong, and being one of only two girls in a class full of boys did not deter her from attending school. She looked forward to going to school every day.

"*Ammani!* It is my dream to see you study well and graduate like Kadambini Ganguly," Keshavamurthy would lovingly tell his little daughter.

"I will, *Appa!*" Kasthuri assured her father with great determination. Kasthuri was in her third year of middle school, which lasted four years. She excelled in her studies, particularly in mathematics, her favourite subject. All her teachers, especially Sir Albert Victor, the school's principal and her math teacher, were immensely fond of the sincere, hardworking Kasthuri.

The couple's youngest child, Bhagwan, was a lovable, mischievous, hyperactive lad. Although he was particularly close to Kasthuri, he also enjoyed bothering her. That morning was no different. As Jalaja was plaiting Kasturi's hair, he grabbed her black-coloured ribbons and ran away, annoying his sister to no end.

"Bhagwan, stop!" Kasthuri screamed and followed her brother as he ran through the corridors of their spacious, ancestral *Thotti Mane*, a traditional old-style Karnataka house with an open-to-sky courtyard at its centre, covered with an iron grill on top to allow sufficient sunlight to seep in. The house was characterised by smoothly polished teakwood pillars surrounding the rectangular courtyard, firmly holding up the terracotta-tiled roof.

Rooms surrounded all three sides of the courtyard, while the front door opened onto a large verandah. A sizable granary was constructed on the right side of the courtyard, next to the entrance. It was typically used to store dried coffee seeds before they were sold and shipped in batches to merchants, and it also served as a perfect hideout for children playing hide-and-seek. The colourful Athangudi tiled flooring gave the house a regal appearance, and a spacious red oxide-tiled kitchen opened into the backyard.

Bhagwan, running away from his sister, bumped into Alamelamma, who was coming out of the kitchen holding the Naivedya vessel in her hand. She gave him a tight whack. "What has got into you, boy? You are getting naughtier by the day," Alamelamma shouted as Bhagwan ran into the backyard and hid behind the giant mango tree.

The spacious backyard was a tranquil space featuring a variety of fruit trees, a large well in the northeast corner, and a couple of lavatories and baths. As was the norm in traditional homes of that time, toilets and baths were typically located outside the house.

Pankaja and Jalaja ran into the backyard with Kasthuri. Together, the three-cornered Bhagwan and caught hold of the naughty boy.

"Got you! Now, give my ribbons back, you irritating brat!" Kasthuri said as she pulled her ribbons from her little brother's hands, not before pinching his ear hard.

By then, Keshavamurthy had tastefully decorated the deities in the puja room with floral garlands, lit the lamps, and offered prayers. The holy chants of the *Vishnu Sahasranamam* and the divine fragrance of incense made the otherwise gloomy morning appear brighter and livelier.

Once the puja was completed, Keshavamurthy walked onto the verandah and settled into his favourite teakwood armchair. A few wicker chairs flanked either side of the armchair, and a wooden plank swing hung to the right of the verandah.

A beautifully built *'Tulasi katte'* painted in red, green, and yellow hues stood in the centre of the front yard. In addition to the well-maintained flower garden, the front yard featured several large trees, the brightest of which was the Gulmohar, which constantly bloomed with fiery red flowers that kept dropping, creating a floral path leading to the house.

Keshavamurthy saw Kasthuri standing on the verandah, looking out at the rain with a pensive expression. *"Ammani,* what is bothering you, dear? You look worried," Keshavamurthy lovingly asked.

"Appa, the rain doesn't seem to stop. The first school period is Sir Albert's Math class, and I don't want to miss it."

"It is only eight now, *Ammani!* And your school starts at half past nine. I'm sure the rain will stop by then, and you will not have to miss your favourite class," Keshavamurthy lovingly assured his daughter.

Kasthuri nodded hopefully, walked into her room, and sat by the window nook overlooking the verandah and front yard. From the window, she saw her mother walking onto the verandah with a tumbler of piping hot filter coffee made from freshly roasted and ground coffee beans from their plantation. Keshavamurthy lovingly held his wife's hand as she handed him the tumbler, looked at her affectionately, and said, "Alamelu, why don't you sit here with me for a few minutes?" Alamelamma gently smiled and sat in a chair next to her husband.

"I am sure they would now speak to each other about the Plantation or Jalaja *Akka* and Pankaja *Akka's* weddings." Kasthuri thought, and she was right.

"The plantation is giving out a good yield this year. The demand for coffee beans is increasing tenfold, thanks to the British and their love for coffee. Suppose all goes well by God's grace, we will make a phenomenal profit this year," Keshavamurthy said, and Alamelamma beamed happily.

"God willing, if we receive good alliances for the girls, we could use a portion of the money to perform their marriages well and save the rest," suggested Alamelamma, who helped her husband efficiently plan the family's finances.

The sound of the wrought iron gate opening disturbed their conversation. "Biligiri *Mama!*" Kasthuri said to herself as she saw the short and stout man walk in. Biligiri Rangan lived across the street, a few houses away from the Iyengar house, with his family. He was a close friend of Keshavamurthy Iyengar, who loved Biligiri like a brother. Since their families had been neighbours for generations, Keshavamurthy had known Biligiri and felt great love and affection for him since the latter was a baby.

Biligiri owned a sweet shop named *Sujata Sweets* near the town bus stand. He was infamous for using adulterated and low-quality ingredients to prepare sweets. People avoided his shop and preferred going to *Srinivasa Sweet Shop,* which was located right across the road and owned by Sampath Kumar Iyengar, a distant relative of Keshavamurthy.

Keshavamurthy often subtly advised, "Biligiri, earning money is important, but even more important is how we earn that money."

"*Anna*, Sampath Kumar of *Srinivasa Sweet Shop* is jealous of my success. Hence, he goes around the town, badmouthing me to bring down my business. I use the best and purest ingredients to make the sweets I sell; trust me, *Anna*!" Biligiri would become defensive, and Keshavamurthy would nod.

In the meantime, the rain began to recede after about half an hour. An excited Kasthuri jumped from the window and ran out of the room, shouting excitedly, *"Amma,* the rain has almost stopped. Could you help me with the sari? I'm getting late for school."

On hearing Kasthuri's excited screams, Alamelamma rushed in to help her little daughter with the sari. "Why do you scream so much, Kasthuri? Learn to speak softly like your sisters," she lovingly chided.

"Amma, the teachers say I shouldn't speak loudly in class. You say I shouldn't speak loudly at home. Is there no place in this world where I can talk freely?" Kasthuri complained dramatically.

Alamelamma smiled softly as she helped her daughter drape the light blue khadi sari. If there was anything Kasthuri disliked about school, it was that she had to wear a saree. At home, she wore a comfortable *Pavadai* and blouse. "Amma, why can't I wear a *Pavadai* to school? I don't like wearing a saree."

"No saree, no school!" Alamelamma declared angrily. Kasthuri did not prolong the conversation lest she invite her mother's ire. Alamelamma then walked back into the kitchen and neatly packed two portions of *Chitranna*, one for Kasthuri and one for little Bhagwan, in freshly cut plantain leaves. She tied the packets firmly with twine and handed them to Kasthuri, who carefully placed them in a jute basket alongside her books.

Though the school was only a few blocks away, Kasthuri found it challenging to walk the way to school while holding her basket and her mischievous brother's hand. The little girl would trip over her saree several times while trying to manage her naughty brother before finally reaching school. It was an unpleasant daily ordeal that Kasthuri dreaded.

Bhagwan made it all the more difficult for his sister by letting go of her hand and running here and there, and it irritated her to no end. Kasthuri would get so angry at times that she would smack him hard, and he would then cry his lungs out, further irritating her.

As they entered the school gate, Kasthuri sighed in relief. "Now run to your class, and don't show me your stupid face until the closing bell rings," she said to Bhagwan, who made a funny face and ran toward his class.

Chapter 2

The school building was large and beautiful, designed in the Colonial style. Ironically, although the country was under British rule, the children felt a strange sense of freedom on the school campus because of its open design, which featured spacious, well-ventilated classrooms and beautifully landscaped lawns. The expansive campus housed a church, the teachers' quarters, and the Principal's bungalow.

There was another girl in Kasthuri's class, which was otherwise full of boys. Juliet belonged to a Protestant family. Her father also owned and managed a coffee estate, and like Keshavamurthy, he was very supportive of girls' education.

As Kasthuri walked towards her classroom, she felt happy to see her dear friend, Juliet, waiting at the door. The two girls neither glanced at the boys nor spoke to them, and vice versa. Hence, the girls would feel lonely and lost if either of them were absent.

"Kasthuri!" cried Juliet. "Why are you so late? I thought you wouldn't turn up today."

"Julie," as she fondly called her friend, "It's all because of that little rascal brother of mine. As if walking with this sari is not enough of a task, the brat must also be held on to, lest he runs away and gets lost," Kasthuri answered.

Juliet started laughing, and Kasthuri joined in. They both entered the classroom as they saw Sir Albert approaching. "Good morning, Sir!" the children wished their teacher in chorus, and Kasthuri's favourite mathematics class began.

Kasthuri and Juliet sat on the same bench, happily chatting and joking during breaks and free time. They were almost inseparable during school.

The teachers at the Hardwicke Mission encouraged students to excel in their studies to be considered for future government employment. The prospect of joining the government seemed appealing and fascinating to the innocent young girls.

"Julie, imagine! When we finish graduation and get a government job, the office would send home a car to fetch us," Kasthuri would dreamily say.

"Yes, Kasthuri, we could dress up in grand sarees, reach the office and give endless instructions in English to those working under us," Juliet added. The girls dreamt happily.

When she returned from school with Bhagwan that afternoon, Kasthuri saw her sisters sitting on the verandah swing and enjoying a snack. "Akka, what are you both eating?" she asked inquisitively.

"Kasthuri! Amma has made *Rava vunde* and *Nippattu*. They are delicious," Pankaja said as she took another bite of the crunchy Nippattu. Kasthuri and Bhagwan ran as fast as they could toward the backyard, pushing each other. They quickly washed their hands, legs, and faces and rushed into the kitchen.

"Amma, I'm hungry!" Kasthuri announced while Bhagwan climbed onto a stool and reached for the brass box where his mother usually stored snacks. He opened it, took out a *vunde*, and gobbled it hurriedly, angering his mother. "Have you not got the slightest patience, *Maga?*"

Once they had eaten and changed into fresh home clothes, Kasthuri and her younger brother played together, chasing each other around the house. Biligiri's children, Sujji and Kittu, soon joined them. Pankaja and Jalaja sat on the swing on the verandah, quietly enjoying watching their two younger siblings have fun.

"Akka, why don't you play with us, too?" Kasthuri pleaded with her sisters, who gently refused to join in.

It was not that Pankaja and Jalaja did not want to join in. However, they feared being scolded by their mother, who disapproved of them running around. According to her, the girls were of marriageable age, and she expected them to conduct themselves with a certain amount of decorum. The twin sisters typically entertained themselves by playing *chauka bara*, a wooden board game, in the evenings.

Just then, Rathna, Alamelamma's younger sister, walked in. She lived two houses away with her elderly parents.

Rathna was a tall, fair-complexioned, attractive lady with long, curly hair that was neatly oiled, plaited, and always adorned with a single red rose. She wore a small, bright red *bindi* on her forehead, a short gold chain around her neck, and a couple of gold bangles to complement her slender hands. Her affectionate and jovial nature made Rathna everyone's favourite.

She worked as a music and dance teacher at Vani Vilasa Girls' School in Hassan and travelled to and from work by bus. Not only was she proficient in dance and music, but she also played the *Veena*. Pankaja Jalaja and Kasthuri learned music from Rathna.

Despite being highly talented and educated, the beautiful Rathna was unmarried. Due to the numerous so-called *doshas* in her horoscope, her parents could not find a suitable groom within the Iyengar community. Marrying outside the community was unheard of in those days, so her parents gave up and resigned to their fate.

"I might have surely done some bad *karma* in my past life, and God is punishing my innocent daughter in return. Otherwise, why wouldn't anyone come forward to marry such a lovely girl?" Her mother would sometimes cry inconsolably.

"*Amma,* I am educated, working as a teacher, and earning a decent salary. I can take care of myself very well. So please do not worry," the brave Rathna would reassure her mother.

Kasthuri was very fond of her aunt and eagerly awaited her visits every evening. She learned both vocal music and dance from her. Rathna also helped Kasthuri with her homework. A voracious reader, Rathna encouraged Kasthuri to read by gifting her books and sharing numerous stories about brave women.

"Kasthuri, life is not always a bed of roses. As you grow up, you may face challenges and hardships. But always remember to keep your head high and face all obstacles with a smile. Never lose courage,"

Kasthuri would lovingly hug her aunt and say, "*Chikkamma*, I feel the bravest when you're with me. Promise me that you will be by my side always!" Rathna would emotionally plant a kiss on little Kasthuri's cheek.

Keshavamurthy came home in the evening after finishing his work at the estate. He rested in his armchair on the verandah as his wife handed him a glass of cool water. Kasthuri jumped onto her father's lap and enthusiastically talked about her day at school. She puzzled him with a new mathematics problem she had learned that day.

"Could you please explain it to me, *Ammani?* No matter how much I think, I don't seem to get it," Keshavamurthy said after pretending to think hard. While Kasthuri enthusiastically solved the problem, the proud father lovingly watched her.

The following morning, as Pankaja was plaiting Kasthuri's hair, the two sisters overheard their father speaking to Biligiri. "Is anything the matter, Biligiri? You seem to be worried!" Keshavamurthy inquired.

"*Anna*, we have been invited to the wedding of Ambujam's distant cousin. Since it's the end of the month, I don't have enough money to gift the newlyweds. But Ambujam is determined to attend the wedding."

"That is hardly a matter to worry so much over," Keshavamurthy said as he brought some money out of the safe and shoved it forcefully into Biligiri's pocket. Due to his dire financial planning, Biligiri often found himself in difficult circumstances. He would ask Keshavamurthy for help without hesitation, and Keshavamurthy readily bailed him out.

"I wonder what Bilgiri *mama* would do without *Appa*," Pankaja remarked as she finished plaiting Kasthuri's hair. Once she was ready, Kasthuri walked into the verandah and sat there waiting for Bhagwan. She listened to the friend duo continue their conversation over hot tumblers of filter coffee that Alamelamma had served them.

Ramaraya Mallya, a freedom fighter, started Satyagrahi, a cyclostyled newspaper, to spread nationalist fervour. Biligiri somehow procured the paper every morning and brought it to Keshavamurthy, who read every word of it with great zeal.

"Biligiri, Gandhiji is addressing a meeting in Bangalore tomorrow to encourage people to participate in the non-cooperation movement against the British."

"Anna, would the British not object to this meeting? Would they permit it to happen?"

"Why not Biligiri? Gandhiji advocates peaceful and non-violent ways of protest. There is no reason why the British should take an objection to such a meeting", answered Keshavamurthy.

As Kasthuri intently listened to their conversation, she was disturbed by Bhagwan calling her, *"Akka!* Let's go!"

A few days later, on a Sunday evening, Narayana came home with some news. *"Appa*, I heard from my friends that there will be a huge bonfire near the Maharaja Circle at the marketplace tonight, organised by Gandhiji's followers, and they are encouraging everyone to discard any British goods that they might have into it," Narayana announced

"Gandhiji spoke about the non-cooperation movement at the Bangalore meeting just last week. I'm so glad his followers are enthusiastically implementing his instructions already," remarked an overjoyed Keshavamurthy. He then looked at Alamelamma and gave out a series of instructions.

"Alamelu, please bring me my black coat, all of Narayana's and Bhagwan's shirts that we got made of British Manchester cloth, the Liverpool salt you have been using in the kitchen, and all other British goods at home." Alamelamma went in obediently and shortly returned with a big bundle.

"We shall throw all of these into the bonfire today. It will be our little way of showing our allegiance to our motherland."

"Appa, I love my green and blue Manchester cloth shirts. I don't want to put them into the fire." Bhagwan said, starting to cry and throwing a tantrum.

"Bhagwan, in place of those two shirts, I promise to buy you four more shirts made of Indian *Khadi*. Do not cry," Keshavamurthy lovingly cajoled and consoled his youngest son.

When Keshavamurthy and his family arrived at the bonfire venue in the evening, a considerable crowd had already gathered. They were tossing British goods they had brought into the fire as they chorused slogans of *'Gandhiji ki jai,'* *'Vande Mataram!' And 'Bharat mata ki jai!'*.

Although the children initially felt shy, they soon joined the crowd enthusiastically with their father, chanting nationalistic slogans. Surprisingly, Bhagwan was the loudest among them and helped his father and brother throw away the things they had brought, including his favourite shirts.

The following day at school, Kasthuri excitedly spoke to Juliet about the previous night's bonfire when Sister Alphonso walked in sternly. Sir Albert entered a few minutes later and announced, "Children, as you might be well aware, several anti-government activities and sloganeering are happening throughout the town. I hereby instruct all students not to participate in or be associated with any such activity, failing which the concerned student will be rusticated."

Shortly after he left the class, Juliet whispered to Kasthuri, "Kasthuri, don't tell anyone that you were part of yesterday's bonfire event. You don't wish to get rusticated, do you?"

Kasthuri nodded silently. "I must talk to Appa about this!" she thought as she walked home with Bhagwan.

"Amma," she called out to her mother. "I'm home," she announced. Her father's friend, Biligiri's wife, Ambujam, was chatting with her mother in the kitchen.

"Kasthuri, go freshen up. Ambujam *Athe* has brought delicious potato *bajjis*," Alamelamma said.

Kasthuri's mouth watered at the mention of bajjis. She rushed to the backyard for a quick wash. As she savoured the *bajjis*, she overheard the conversation between her mother and Ambujam.

"*Akka*, we have been invited to a wedding, and I have no decent jewellery to wear to the wedding. Could I borrow your ruby necklace for a day? I promise to take care of it and return it as soon as I come back from the wedding," requested Ambujam

"By all means, Ambujam! I will surely give it to you after I speak with my husband," Alamelamma assured. After a few minutes, Ambujam left.

Kasthuri did not appreciate Ambujam endlessly borrowing things from her mother, from small items like salt and sugar to more expensive ones, such as necklaces and silk sarees. "Amma, why does Ambujam *athe* keep borrowing things from us?"

"Kasthuri, it's not a good habit to meddle in the affairs of elders. Biligiri *Mama* is more than a brother to *Appa*. *Appa* would be saddened if he were to know that you were badmouthing Ambujam *Athe*." The anger in her mother's tone silenced Kasthuri, and she continued to eat without saying another word.

"Now! If you're done eating, go and play with your brother," Alamelamma said sternly. Kasthuri suddenly missed Rathna, who was away in Mysore attending a wedding.

Keshavamurthy came home late evening, and Kasthuri rushed to the gate to greet her father. She held his hand as they walked toward the house.

"Appa, could you sit for a while? I need to speak to you about something serious!" Kasthuri requested.

"Why are such serious matters troubling my little child?" Keshavamurthy remarked in good humour as he sat in his armchair and pulled his darling daughter onto his lap. Kasthuri told her father about Sir Albert's warning to the students.

"Appa, we aren't doing anything wrong in fighting for our independence, are we?".

"No. Not at all, *Ammani;* it is just that with the freedom struggle gaining momentum all over the country, the British are now getting worried and feeling insecure that they might eventually lose control over our country. Hence, such warnings and announcements."

"What if Albert Sir learns that I was also at the bonfire event that evening? Would he rusticate me?".

"None can rusticate you or anyone for just peacefully standing there."

"What if they do, *appa?*" Kasthuri was still worried.

"In such a case, I would join you at Vani Vilasa Girls' School, and you could go to school every day with *Chikkamma.* All right?"

Her father's reassurance brightened Kasthuri's face, bringing her a sense of relief.

Chapter 3

It was a bright Sunday morning, and Keshavamurthy did not go to the estate on Sundays; he preferred to stay home and spend time with his family. Sunday was also the day of *Abhyanga snana*, or the traditional oil bath. Alamelammaa handed bowls of warm sesame oil to each of them, which they were to apply and massage onto their heads and entire bodies. The hair would then be washed using the froth from boiled *reetha* seeds.

"Amma, my eyes are burning!" Bhagwan started to howl.

"Didn't I tell you to close your eyes, *Maga?* Hold on, it's almost done!" Alamelamma quickly washed Bhagwan's hair.

"Amma, why do you make us endure this routine every Sunday? Is there nothing better than this bitter-tasting, nasty froth to wash our hair?" Kasthuri complained as her mother rinsed her long, lustrous hair.

The children's ordeal was far from over. Once they had all bathed and dressed, Alamelamma handed them small balls of neem leaves and turmeric to swallow with warm water. Thus, the Sunday morning rituals were completed, despite the younger children's resistance and tantrums.

"Pankaja, cut these vegetables for me, will you? Jalaja, hurry up and grate the coconut," she instructed her older daughters as she busied herself preparing a special Sunday meal for her family. The day's delicacies included potato fry, drumstick and tomato *sambar*, *Tili saaru, payasam*, rice, and curds. The whole family sat together and enjoyed the sumptuous meal that Alamelamma had lovingly prepared.

"Alamelu, there is indeed magic in your hands that makes every dish you make taste heavenly," Keshavamurthy complimented his wife as he relished the rice *payasam*, and the children agreed.

Alamelamma was an expert cook who never took shortcuts but painstakingly and lovingly followed the elaborate and detailed cooking procedures she had learned from her mother and grandmother. She did not believe in preparing and storing her *sambar* and *rasam* powders, as she strongly felt that the longer these powders were stored, the less aroma and flavour they would retain; therefore, she would hand-grind them as needed. Needless to say, the dishes she prepared tasted heavenly.

Relatives and friends often complimented Keshavamurthy on how lucky he was to have such a perfect homemaker for a wife. In response, Keshavamurthy would lift his hands upwards as though thanking the universe and say with a contented smile, "I'm blessed indeed to have Alamelu as my wife."

Keshavamurthy had noticed that his wife seemed dull and withdrawn since morning. After lunch, they sat on the verandah, watching the children play. "Alamelu, you seem unusually quiet today. What is bothering you?" Keshavamurthy asked cajolingly.

Alamelu initially brushed off the question, saying it was nothing. However, as Keshavamurthy pressed further, Alamelu responded, "If you recall, Ambujam had borrowed my ruby necklace to wear to a wedding almost ten days ago. She promised to return it to me the next day, but hasn't returned it yet," Alamelamma said.

"She might have forgotten amidst her work and the children. Let us wait a few more days".

"It is a precious heirloom piece given to me by your mother, and I hope it is safe. I am starting to get worried," she said. Keshavamurthy thought briefly and then called Narayana.

"Please go to Biligiri *Chikkappa's* house and subtly remind them to return *Amma's* necklace."

Narayana went and returned in a few minutes. "*Appa*, Bilgiri *Chikkappa* said he would come and hand it over in a few minutes."

In about half an hour, Bilgiri came in smiling and handed the necklace to Alamelamma, apologising profusely.

"*Athige,* please forgive us for the delay in returning the necklace. Kittu has not been feeling well, hence the delay," Bilgiri pleaded.

"That's okay, Biligiri," Alamelamma said, heaving a sigh of relief.

Sunday evenings were typically a time for family gatherings. By 5:30 pm, Biligiri and his family arrived at the Iyengar house. Rathna and her parents had returned from the Mysore wedding the previous day, and they, too, came to Keshavamurthy's house that evening. The children squealed with delight as they surrounded their aunt, who lovingly gave them the toys and sweets she had brought from Mysore.

Alamelamma was frying the last batch of *goli bajjis* when Rathna and Ambujam joined her in the kitchen. As she took a generous bite of the hot *bajji*, Ambujam excitedly shared the latest gossip she had gathered about the women living in the nearby houses.

Rathna, a woman of impeccable character and high moral values, thoroughly disliked listening to Ambujam speak ill of others and gossip behind their backs. However, she never expressed her feelings, fearing it would anger her brother-in-law. Keshavamurthy's deep affection for Biligiri and his wife was known to all.

Outside, in the living room, the three men had now shifted to discussing the British atrocities, the heavy taxes they imposed, and the freedom movement that was in full swing across the country. The extremists were gaining traction in the nation, which Keshavamurthy and many from his generation disapproved of. "Violence can never help us gain independence. The extremists and their violent ways, will make the British even more stubborn", he opined, while others agreed.

Meanwhile, steaming hot bajjis were now ready to be served. As they all sat down to savour the soft and spicy goli bajjis, Kamalamma, Alamelamma's mother, brought up the topic of her twin granddaughters' weddings.

"Keshava, do you remember Sarojini, my Chikamma's daughter-in-law, who lives in Bangalore? She has two sons who recently graduated and secured government jobs. She is looking for suitable girls for them."

"Both boys attended the wedding in Mysore and are extremely respectful, well-mannered, and presentable. It would be a suitable alliance for Pankaja and Jalaja. Since the boys are brothers, our girls can happily stay together in the same house."

Keshavamurthy seemed pleased. Saroja's late husband, Devarajan, was well-known to Keshavamurthy until he unexpectedly passed away from a massive heart attack.

Kamalamma looked at Keshavamurthy and continued, "I informed Saroja that we are also looking for suitable boys for our Pankaja and Jalaja. I had the photos of the girls in my bag and showed them to her. She seemed highly impressed and interested in taking the matter forward."

"Pankaja and Jalaja would be fortunate to step into Devarajan's house as daughters-in-law. Let us pray that things go well and this alliance is fixed," Keshavamurthy hoped.

Everyone seemed happy with the pleasant development. Pankaja and Jalaja, sitting nearby and overhearing the conversation, blushed and ran inside.

A month later, on an auspicious day, Keshavamurthy and Alamelamma conducted the weddings of their older daughters to the best of their abilities. After bidding an emotional farewell to their family, the girls left for Bangalore with their husbands.

The Iyengar house was suddenly bereft of Pankaja and Jalaja's vibrant presence, and everyone greatly missed them.

"Julie, I miss Pankaja *Akka* oiling and plaiting my hair every morning. I miss seeing them sitting on the swing every afternoon, waiting for Bhagwan and me to come home from school. I also miss watching them make those beautiful garlands for the deities. Oh! I truly miss my sisters." Kasthuri shared her feelings with Juliet, and her eyes welled up with tears.

Chapter 4

Kasthuri was now 12 and had been promoted to the fourth year of middle school. She excelled in all subjects and earned top marks. Bhagwan was 10 and in the second year of middle school. He was his usual mischievous self, but was doing reasonably well in school.

A few days later, Keshavamurthy received a wedding invitation from his older sister, Ahalya, and her husband, who lived in Madras, inviting Keshavamurthy and his family to their son's wedding. Since it was difficult for everyone to travel that far, Keshavamurthy decided to attend the wedding alone.

As the day of his travel approached, Keshavamurthy became concerned about the well-being of the estate during his absence. Narayana was quite irresponsible, while the workers needed careful supervision.

"Narayana, I expect you to act responsibly and care well for the estate in my absence. I have also asked Biligiri to assist you," Keshavamurthy said, to which Narayana nodded.

"Alamelu, do not forget to lock all the doors at night cautiously, and do not let any stranger inside the compound." He instructed his wife. He had the utmost confidence in Alamelamma's capabilities. On the home front, he felt reassured. The only worry was the well-being of the estate. Finally, the day of travel arrived, and Keshavamurthy started on his journey.

A week later, when he returned home from Madras, Alamelamma and the children, especially Kasthuri, were ecstatic. However, Keshavamurthy appeared extremely tired and forlorn. Initially, Alamelamma thought her husband might be exhausted from the long and tiring journey. She reassured herself that he would be fine after a few days of rest. Nevertheless, Keshavamurthy's condition began to deteriorate. He experienced bloody diarrhoea and vomiting accompanied by a high fever.

A worried Alamelamma sent Narayana to fetch Dr. Rangachary, a well-known Ayurvedic doctor and their family physician. After a detailed examination, he declared that Keshavamurthy seemed to have contracted cholera. Cholera was rampant in Madras at that time, and the doctor suspected Keshavamurthy might have contracted the illness during his trip to Madras. Alamelamma broke down crying as the children surrounded their mother with tense, gloomy faces.

Dr. Rangachari assured Alamelamma that Keshavamurthy's condition was treatable.

"Alamelamma, a strict diet and the right medicines are needed to control the illness," the doctor advised.

"Only rice with water-rich vegetables, such as gourds, and non-spicy vegetable broths must be given. Juices and buttermilk should also be given at regular intervals to prevent dehydration," he instructed.

Kasthuri often stood at the door of her father's room where he slept and watched him silently. The sight of her frail and ailing father broke her heart. She rushed to her room and broke down. "Oh, Lord Venkataramana! Make my father healthy again!" she would pray.

Rathna, Biligiri, and Ambujam provided great strength and support during this time. Biligiri also assured that he would help Narayana manage the estate in Keshavamurthy's absence, greatly relieving Keshavamurthy.

Narayana returned to his old ways in his father's absence. "It's high time you acted with a sense of responsibility, at least now when your father is so ill. Go see what is happening at the estate at least once a day," Alamelamma pleaded with her son, who turned a deaf ear.

In a couple of weeks, thanks to the doctor's efforts and Alamelammas's round-the-clock personal care, Keshavamurthy's fever began responding to the treatment, and Dr. Rangachari was pleased with the improvement.

Alamelamma was leaving no stone unturned in nursing her husband back to health. However, the financial situation was a cause for concern. Huge expenses had recently been incurred for the twins' weddings, and a substantial amount of money was now spent on Keshavamurthy's treatment and household expenses.

"The cash in the safe is dwindling. We do not have much money left in the safe," Alamelamma reluctantly told her husband.

"The yield at the estate will take at least six more months to be harvested and sold. Now that we have almost run out of the liquid cash I had kept aside, the only option is to sell the plot of land in Hassan," Keshavamurthy said after some thinking, much to the disappointment of Alamelamma, who was not in favour of selling any of their properties. However, there was no option either.

Biligiri assisted people in selling and purchasing land, earning a commission in return. At Keshavamurthy's request, Biligiri promptly brought in an interested party within a week.

"Anna, the prospective buyers like the plot of land very much and wish to complete the registration formalities exactly a week from now as per their astrologer's advice," Biligiri said.

"I am still too weak to even stand for a few minutes. Narayana cannot sign on my behalf since he is officially not yet an adult. Alamelu is not worldly-wise. Going through the registration formalities would be a big deal for her, and she might panic", Keshavamurthy thought to himself. Rathna's name crossed his mind, but somehow, his ego did not permit him to ask for help from his sister-in-law. He also felt it would not be wise to disturb his sons-in-law. "Then how could the registration be done?" he thought. The only person who came to Keshavamurthy's mind was Biligiri. He trusted Biligiri as much as he would trust his brother.

"You, Biligiri, are all I can think of to help me in this situation. You know that I trust you more than anyone in this world. Please do the registration formalities on my behalf."

"I consider it my great fortune to be of some help to you, *Anna*. I would be more than happy to complete the registration formalities on your behalf."

Biligiri promptly had the power of attorney document drafted and ready in a few days. Biligiri and the assistant sub-registrar arrived at Keshavamurthy's house with the document. The official handed it to Keshavamurthy and explained, "This is the 'General Power of Attorney,' which will enable the bearer, Biligiri, in this case, to buy, sell, and register property on your behalf." Keshavamurthy nodded in agreement.

"I would advise that once the registration formality of this property is completed, the document needs to be taken back, and the General Power of Attorney bestowed upon Biligiri needs to be officially cancelled. Am I clear?" he asked, and Keshavamurthy nodded in affirmation. Then, as guided by the official, Keshavamurthy signed at marked places. Biligiri and Narayana went to the sub-registrar's office the next day to register the document. They later handed it over to Keshavamurthy, who instructed his wife to keep it carefully.

On the day of registration, after completing the formalities, the buyers handed Narayana the agreed amount. Biligiri and Narayana then returned home and promptly gave the amount to Keshavamurthy.

"Thank you, *Kano*, for helping us at the right time." Keshavamurthy profusely thanked Biligiri for his help.

"Come, have lunch with us, Biligiri," Alamelamma invited.

Biligiri rushed out in a hurry, saying, "*Athige*, I have important work to do. Since I'm already running late, I promise to return in the evening and relish everything you have prepared. For now, please excuse me."

Keshavamurthy happily handed the amount to Alamelamma to be kept in the iron Safe.

"Narayana, please also hand over the GPA document to Amma. We need to apply for the cancellation as soon as possible."

"*Appa*, I do not have the GPA document. It is probably still with Biligiri Chikkappa," Narayana answered.

"Biligiri was in a hurry and might have forgotten to hand over the document. He said he would come by this evening. We can collect the document then," Keshavamurthy said confidently.

As expected, Biligiri came that evening and handed over the document, apologising for not doing so earlier.

Keshavamurthy was improving day by day. In a couple of weeks, he could walk comfortably around the house and sit in his armchair for a while. Doctor Rangachari, encouraged by this progress in his patient, instructed Alamelamma to begin a regular diet, as there had been no fever or diarrhoea for the past ten days. Keshavamurthy was now able to enjoy meals with his family.

"I wonder why none of the estate workers have come to see me. Have they not been informed of my illness?" Keshavamurthy sounded puzzled.

"Appa, I had seen Ramanna and Ganesha at our gate several times. But they were reprimanded and sent away by Biligiri Mama," Kasthuri recollected.

Alamelamma added, "I, too, have seen Ramanna being sent away by Biligiri a couple of times."

"I wonder why Biligiri would do that!" Keshavamurthy pondered. "He probably did not want me to be disturbed," he later concluded.

Another week passed, and Biligiri continued to manage the estate's affairs. When he went to see Keshavamurthy that morning, he was pleasantly surprised to find him sitting in his armchair on the verandah, looking bright and cheerful. "It feels so good to see you back to being healthy and happy, *Anna,*" Biligiri said.

"Thanks to you, Biligiri, for taking care of everything while I was unwell," Keshavamurthy said, looking at Biligiri affectionately. "I am planning to start visiting the estate from the day after," Keshavamurthy added, to which Biligiri nodded absentmindedly. Early the next morning, Biligiri entered Keshavamurthy's house in a hurry, looking tense.

"Anna, my sister Pushpa's husband, has had a major road accident. He is admitted to a hospital in Mysore and is in a critical state, " Bilgiri explained anxiously. He planned to leave for Mysore that very night along with his family. He had come to seek Keshavamurthy's blessings before doing so.

"You travel safely and write to me when you have time. Don't hesitate to let me know if you need any money for hospital expenses," Keshavamurthy graciously offered.

Chapter 5

The next day, after nearly six weeks of illness, Keshavamurthy got ready to visit his estate, feeling happy and eager to set foot on it again. "Narayana, hurry up! Will you?" he rushed his lethargic son. For some reason, it was a holiday at school, and the younger children were also at home. Kasthuri insisted on going with her father, and Keshavamurthy agreed after initially being reluctant.

As the three of them entered the estate, they were surprised to see a robust, middle-aged man with a bushy moustache sitting in Keshavamurthy's chair, instructing the workers, who appeared to be newly appointed. None of the old, trusted workers were in sight. The father-son duo was shocked to see this man wielding authority in their estate. As they walked towards him, the man looked at them questioningly.

"Sir, who are you, and what do you want?" the man asked.

"I am Keshavamurthy, the owner of this estate. May I know who you are and what you're doing here?" Keshavamurthy asked. The man sprang up from his chair in shock and disbelief.

"Are you in your senses? Biligiri sold this estate to me a month back for a fortune. I am the new owner of the estate."

Keshavamurthy felt himself sinking into the ground in disbelief. Narayana and Kasthuri were also stunned beyond words. Narayana clutched his father's hand, fearing he might fall.

"I'm the whole and sole owner of this estate. This is my ancestral property. How can anybody sell it to you? Your claim is illegal, and I shall file a case against you," Keshavamurthy shouted angrily.

"This property has been registered in my name in the sub-registrar office in the presence of the Registrar. Go ahead and file a case. I shall file a case against you for trespassing on my property and threatening me," the man shouted. He instructed the workers to force Keshavamurthy and the children out of the estate and to close the gate.

On being pushed out of his ancestral property, Keshavamurthy collapsed and wailed loudly. "Biligiri, you rascal! What have you done? How did you have the heart to cheat me?" he cried.

Pained by their father's helpless condition, Kasthuri and Narayana, too, began to cry inconsolably. Narayana soon regained his composure and persuaded his father that they should return home and consider what must be done. Keshavamurthy managed to get up with great difficulty and went home with Narayana and Kasthuri supporting him on either side, still weeping loudly.

Upon hearing her husband's cries, Alamelamma rushed out, only to find Keshavamurthy distressed. With Narayana's help, she assisted her husband into his armchair. She asked

Bhagwan to hurry to Ratha's house and bring them along immediately. She offered her husband a glass of water, but he refused.

Rathna and her parents rushed in, wondering what had happened. Upon entering, they were shocked to see Keshavamurthy weeping uncontrollably while hitting his head with his hands.

"What happened, Narayana? Why is *Bava* devastated?" asked a concerned Rathna.

"*Chikkamma*, Biligiri mama has cheated us. He sold our estate to Someone else without our knowledge," Narayana explained amidst sobs. Rathna and her parents were shocked and petrified as well.

Alamelamma was inconsolable."Biligiri, we treated you like our son. How could you do this to us? Aren't you even scared of God's wrath?" she cried.

It tore at Kasthuri's heart to see her parents in so much pain, and she felt helpless. Little Bhagwan had never seen his father cry, and the sight of him wailing heartbreakingly scared him, causing him to hold on to Kasthuri tightly.

"The rascal had the GPA document with him until evening. He might have used the document to register the estate during the gap between the registration of our plot and the time until evening. How foolish of me to have trusted that snake more than I would trust my kith and kin," a weeping Keshavamurthy said.

Everyone was shocked and terrified to learn how meticulously Biligiri had planned everything right under their noses. Rathna and Narayana caught the next bus to Mysore and took a horse cart straight to Pushpa's house. Pushpa was shocked and ashamed to hear about what her brother had done. "My husband is doing absolutely fine. Biligiri has lied to you," she said. It was clear that Biligiri was absconding with the money. Rathna and Narayana returned home by evening from Mysore, feeling dejected.

The following day, Rathna accompanied Keshavamurthy to meet with lawyer Vasudeva. After hearing the entire story, the lawyer stated that he would file a case, but could not guarantee a victory since Keshavamurthy himself had signed the GPA.

"The GPA is a powerful legal document, and no one can contest its legality," the lawyer stated. As expected, Keshavamurthy Iyengar lost his case and his ancestral estate.

"If I had been more responsible and interested in the estate's affairs, Bilgiri would not have been able to cheat us. Instead of being of help to my parents in trying times, I chose to be irresponsible." Narayana thought as he was swept with feelings of extreme guilt and shame.

"Forgive me, *Appa!*" Crying loudly, he fell at his father's feet, who quietly lifted him, holding his shoulders. Without saying a word, Keshavamurthy walked into his room. He kept to himself and stayed in his room all day.

"*Appa,* you haven't eaten anything since morning. Shall I get you a glass of milk at least?" a worried Kasthuri asked her father. Keshavamurthy nodded in refusal and closed his eyes as he lay on his bed. It pained Kasthuri to see her disconsolate father, and she walked out of the room, wiping away the tears that flowed down her cheeks.

"Julie, Bilgiri *Chikkappa* has cheated us and sold our plantation estate to Someone else, and my parents have been shattered ever since." Kasthuri cried her heart out to Juliet at school the next day. The news shocked Juliet, too, as she knew of the close bond between Biligiri and Kasthuri's father.

"Do not worry, Kasthuri. I'm sure Biligiri will return to his senses and return the money to your father." Juliet tried to console a disturbed Kasthuri

Sharing her feelings with her friend and hearing her comforting words helped Kasthuri feel better. The atmosphere at home was dull and depressing, so coming to school offered Kasthuri some respite.

As they entered the gate of their house that evening, Kasthuri saw her father sitting in his armchair, appearing distraught and dishevelled. Her heart felt heavy as she looked at him. She slowly walked toward him, took his hand, and spoke softly.

"*Appa,* you neither speak nor smile these days, and it breaks my heart to see you like this," she said, starting to sob uncontrollably. His daughter's words moved Keshavamurthy. He looked up at her with tears in his eyes and patted her cheek lovingly.

"*Ammani*! My darling! Don't worry. Appa will be fine in a few days. Go freshen up and eat something," he said lovingly.

Meanwhile, Keshavamurthy's childhood friend and distant relative, Ramanujan, who lived in Mysore, visited Keshavamurthy after hearing from a relative how Biligiri had cheated him.

"Keshava, whatever happened is indeed sad, but there is no point in dwelling on it. For the sake of your family, you need to get hold of yourself and march into the future with hope."

"Everything is lost, Ramanuja. There is nothing left to look forward to!" a dejected Keshavamurthy said with a choked voice.

Ramanuja lovingly comforted and consoled Keshavamurthy. Ramanuja was a wealthy man who owned a well-known coffee shop in Mysore. He offered to take Narayana along and train him in the business, and Keshavamurthy readily agreed. The following day, Ramanuja left for Mysore with Narayana in tow.

Now that the daily routine of visiting the plantation was no longer necessary, Keshavamurthy felt a sudden emptiness. He did not know what to do with his time or how to keep himself engaged, and his idleness made him sadder.

Kasthuri came home from school that day, jumping with joy. *"Appa*, our progress reports have been given today. Guess what? I have stood first in all the subjects in my class. During the morning school assembly, Sir Albert felicitated me in front of the whole school and presented me with this shield." Kasthuri proudly showed her father the shiny shield she had been awarded.

Keshavamurthy lovingly made Kasthuri sit on his lap and gently kissed her cheek. He happily touched the shield over and over again.

"I'm extremely proud of you, *Ammani!* You are indeed blessed abundantly by the goddess Saraswati. I wish to see you become a graduate one day and win many more accolades, my darling," said an overwhelmed Keshavamurthy. He sat in the armchair holding the shield until late evening, when Kasthuri called him in for dinner.

"*Appa,* dinner is served. Please come in."

"I'm not hungry, *Ammani.* Could you get me a glass of hot milk instead?"

Keshavamurthy went to bed soon after finishing the glass of milk Kasthuri had given him. The following morning, Kasthuri was rudely awakened by her mother's wails and ran to her father's room. Her father lay motionless on his bed, and her mother frantically tried to wake him. Kasthuri, too, joined her mother in waking him. *"Appa!* Wake up!" she called repeatedly, but her father did not respond and remained still.

Soon, Rathna, her parents, and a few neighbours gathered. One of the neighbours rushed to bring in Dr. Rangachari, who promptly arrived, checked on Keshavamurthy, and informed the family that Keshavamurthy had left this world. Alamelamma refused to believe the doctor.

"My husband did not eat anything last night. He is probably just unconscious. Please recheck him," she frantically requested of the doctor, who nodded helplessly, folded his hands, and left. Alamelamma was inconsolable, and her heartwrenching cries made everyone present emotional, too.

The sad news of Keshavamurthy's sudden demise was shared with relatives and friends. The two older girls arrived with their families. Ramanuja brought along an inconsolable Narayana, who clung to his father's feet and cried bitterly, begging for forgiveness. None could pacify him.

The funeral was a painful affair. With the support of relatives and friends, Narayana, with tears of guilt and sorrow continuously flowing down his cheeks, completed the funeral rituals and bid a final farewell to his father. The house seemed to be orphaned of Keshavamurthy's strong, reassuring presence.

Kasthuri missed her father dearly. Every corner of the house and every room reminded Kasthuri of him, and his memory made her cry. She remembered how her father would lovingly call her *"Ammani,"* which again brought tears to her eyes.

A few days later, a dejected Kasthuri sat by the window nook in her room, overlooking the verandah. As she gazed out the window at her father's armchair, Kasthuri was reminded of him and his last wish, which he had expressed while sitting in that chair — the wish to see her graduate. The memory remained so fresh that it caused her immense pain when it crossed her mind.

When Narayana noticed his sister mourning silently, his heart went out to her. He suggested, "Kasthuri, I feel it's high time you and Bhagwan start attending school again. It will make you both feel better." Kasthuri readily accepted her brother's suggestion, as home reminded her of her dear father every moment.

As a few months passed, things began to stabilise slowly at the Iyengar household. A year rolled by quickly, and Kasthuri was now 13 years old. She had been promoted to the fourth form and, as always, was doing very well in school. Bhagwan was now 11 years old and in the third year of middle school. Narayana was working hard at his job in Mysore. Pankaja's husband worked as a government employee in Bangalore, while Jalaja's husband, who worked in the Railways department, had moved to Delhi on deputation for two years.

With the estate gone, no steady income came in. Narayana was not earning enough to support his family back home. Alamelamma had worried about her family's financial future. She shared her concerns with Rathna, who suggested starting a small-scale home food business.

Alamelamma was now busy for most of the day, roasting and grinding spices for sambar and rasam powders while also making a variety of sweets and savouries. Seeing her mother return to her active, enthusiastic self made Kasthuri extremely happy.

Thanks to Rathna's marketing efforts and her family's support, Alamelamma's small-scale business began to gain momentum slowly but steadily. Orders gradually started pouring in, and Alamelamma saved a decent amount each month, which helped cover most household expenses. This provided Alamelamma with a sense of relief and empowerment as she placed the month's savings in the tin box.

Meanwhile, Pankaja, who was in her third trimester of pregnancy, returned home for her delivery. Under her mother's expert and loving care, Pankaja's pregnancy progressed well, and she felt the baby's movements more intensely and regularly. Kasthuri and Bhagwan often placed their hands on their sister's tummy, jumping for joy whenever they could feel the baby kick.

"Julie, my sister, will surely give birth to a wrestler. You must feel his kicks to believe what I say," Kasthuri told her friend happily. Both friends would then laugh heartily.

After completing her full term, Pankaja gave birth to a healthy baby boy, bringing much joy to both families. The baby, now three months old, was named Govind, and it was soon time for Pankaja and Govind to leave for Bangalore.

Chapter 6

Narayana had been working hard and doing very well at his job. He had gradually started to learn the nuances of the business and put his heart and soul into his work. The shop was already thriving, but Narayana helped elevate its fame and business to new heights. They moved to newer, more spacious premises. New coffee-making machines were also purchased to cater to the growing customer base. The new shop even included a spacious seating area where customers could enjoy freshly brewed coffee.

Ramanuja was amazed by Narayana's transformation from a reckless, irresponsible boy to a mature, hardworking, and savvy businessman. Narayana had also become more responsible at home. He visited Sakleshpur once a month for a couple of days and took good care of his family. Alamelamma wished her husband were alive to see how efficiently and responsibly their son was handling all matters now.

Kasthuri and Bhagwan performed well in school, although Bhagwan often needed reminders to complete his work on time. He would lose track of time and come home late after playing with his friends, often sitting in tears as he realised he had a lot of homework to do. Kasthuri would then help her little brother.

"Bhagwan, this is the last time I'll do your homework. Next time, I shall tell your teacher myself that you play all the time," she would warn.

The next afternoon, Alamelamma received a telegram from Saroja: "Jalaja blessed with twins—a boy and a girl. Both mother and babies are safe." Alamelamma's joy knew no bounds. That day was nothing short of a grand celebration at the Iyengar household.

A few days later, when Kasthuri returned home from school, she saw her mother sitting on the swing, appearing dull and lost in thought. She placed her basket on the floor and joined her mother on the swing.

"Amma, you seem to be feeling dejected for some reason. What is the matter?"

"Nothing, my darling! Why don't you go freshen up and eat something? I have saved some *Avalakki* mixture from today's order. Go help yourself and give some to your brother, too."

"Amma, I can see that you're worried about something. You can share your feelings with me. I am old enough to understand."

Alamelamma had always considered and treated Kasthuri and Bhagwan as her little babies. She was pleasantly surprised to realise how grown-up and mature her darling girl had become.

"Kasthuri, I am sad I couldn't be by Jalaja *Akka's* side and care for her during her pregnancy. Jalaja and her babies have been on my mind since this morning."

"*Amma*, I understand how much you miss Jalaja *Akka*. She will be back with us in a few months. You could then pamper her as much as you wish," Kasthuri lovingly cheered her mother, and her words made Alamelamma feel lighter.

In the meantime, the school where Rathna worked, Vani Vilasa Girls' School in Hassan, was one of the many schools and colleges run by the then Maharaja of Mysore. Every year, a group of children from her school would perform during the annual Dasara festivities at the Mysore Palace. Rathna, the dance and music teacher at the school, was responsible for preparing the children for the event. She asked the headmaster if Kasthuri could also be part of this group since she danced very well. After some reluctance, the headmaster agreed.

"Kasthuri! Our headmaster has agreed to let you join us as part of our student group to perform at the Mysore Palace." Rathna gave Kasthuri the good news.

Kasthuri was so happy that she danced around, shrieking with delight. Kasthuri had seen a picture of the Royal Palace, and it was her dream to visit Mysore and witness the magnificent Palace in all its glory. She was so excited that she could hardly sleep that night.

The following day, as the children waited in the classroom for Sister Alphonso, the English teacher, a stern-looking man entered the class instead. "I am Andrew, your new English teacher," he introduced himself to a surprised class.

"I would like to know all of your names, too. Why don't you introduce yourselves, children?" he said after the children had settled down. The children stood up and introduced themselves one by one.

"Sir, my name is Vighnesh," the boy sitting in the front row said.

"And what does your name mean, Vighnesh?"

"Sir! It is one of the names of Lord Ganesha."

"Okay, next!"

"Sir, my name is Shankar," the next boy introduced himself. "It is one of the names of Lord Shiva," he added enthusiastically even before the teacher asked.

"Multiple Gods with multiple names. Rubbish!" teacher Andrew ridiculed sarcastically. Another day, he pointed to a boy in the middle row and asked, "What is that on your forehead?"

"Sir, it is *Vibhuthi*, a sacred ash," the boy explained sincerely.

"Sacred ash! Rubbish! I do not want to see you smearing that disgusting ash and sitting in my class starting tomorrow. Am I clear?" he warned the poor boy.

Teacher Andrew often ridiculed and criticised the children for their religious beliefs. This behaviour eventually became a daily ordeal, much to the students' displeasure.

That evening, as Rathna came home, she found Kasthuri sitting on the verandah steps, deep in thought.

"What happened to my bubbly Kasthuri today?" Rathna asked fondly.

"*Chikkamma*, there is a new teacher named Andrew who has joined in place of Sister Alphonso. He teaches well but wastes half the class time glorifying Christianity and ridiculing other religions."

"*Ayyo*! I wonder why he does that! Did you share your concern with Sir Albert?"

"I don't know if Sir Albert would appreciate me complaining to him about a teacher."

"Does he indulge in criticism of other religions every day?"

"Yes, all the time! Today, he handed everyone a copy of the Holy Bible and instructed us to learn one verse a day by heart and recite it each day at the start of the class, failing which he warned us that he would make us kneel on the floor for the rest of the class," she said and showed Rathna the copy of the Holy Bible.

"What do you plan to do then, Kasturi?" Rathna asked. She was careful not to say anything that might influence her niece.

"I do not know, *Chikkamma,*" Kasthuri answered in a dull tone. The two slowly returned to their dance practice.

The next day in class, teacher Andrew asked each student to stand up and recite the verse they had been assigned to learn. All the children had learned it out of fear of their teacher and recited it sincerely. When it was Kasthuri's turn, she stood up, looked at the teacher, and said, "I did not learn it, Sir."

"Why?" Teacher Andrew was furious.

"I did not have the wish to learn it, Sir," she answered honestly. All the students looked at Kasthuri with expressions of shock.

"How dare you disobey my instructions! Please leave my class immediately. You may be allowed to enter only after learning and reciting the verse without error. Get out now!" Teacher Andrew was furious.

Kasthuri felt insulted and embarrassed as she walked out of the class. Out of helplessness came a sense of courage. She approached the Principal's cabin with her head held high and knocked on the door.

"Sir, may I be permitted to come in"? she asked.

Sir Albert looked up from his papers and saw Kasthuri at the door.

"Kasthuri! Come in! Why are you not in your classroom? What brings you here?"

"Sir, teacher Andrew asked me to leave the class because I did not learn a verse from the Holy Bible."

"Why did you not learn it then, my child?"

"Sir, I sincerely believe that learning the Holy Bible should be a personal choice. It shouldn't be forced upon anyone, just as learning and reciting the shlokas of the Holy Geetha should not be forced upon an unwilling person."

"Are you averse to reading the Holy Bible, Kasthuri?"

"Not at all, Sir! I revere the Holy Bible as much as I revere the Holy Geetha. However, when I wish to read the

Holy Bible, I would want to do it voluntarily; I am only opposed to   force." Sir Albert was amazed and impressed by the clarity of thought and confidence of a young 13-year-old child.

"Very well then! Get back to your class, Child! He then wrote a note to be handed to teacher Andrew. Sir Albert smiled as Kasthuri thanked him and walked toward her class, the note in hand. The next day, Sir Albert walked into class with teacher Andrew.

"Good morning, Sir," the children said in chorus.

"Very good morning, children! Please take your seats! I have been told that teacher Andrew has asked you to learn verses from the Holy Bible. I would like to know how many of you have learned the verses out of your free will and not out of sheer fear of punishment."

The children remained tight-lipped, looking at teacher Andrew with fearful eyes. Teacher Andrew glared at them angrily. Noticing this, Sir Victor politely asked Teacher Andrew to join them in a few minutes. After he left, Sir Victor turned to the students and repeated the question.

"Children, I assure you that your honest answer will be highly appreciated, and there will be no punishment for speaking the truth. Now, I would like all those students who have willingly learned the verses by heart to raise their hands." Except for Juliet, none of the children raised their hands.

"Very well then! I shall instruct Teacher Andrew not to impose upon you the learning of the Biblical verses."

"Thank you, Sir," the children said in chorus as they stood up respectfully. Though teacher Andrew had been indifferent and cold toward Kasthuri for a few days, his attitude eventually changed when he realised she was a brilliant, sincere, and hardworking student.

The day Kasthuri had been eagerly anticipating had finally arrived. It was time to leave for Mysore. Alamelamma had never permitted Kasthuri to travel anywhere without her. She gave Kasthuri endless instructions while packing her clothes and snacks for the trip.

"Kasthuri, do not wander away from the group in your excitement. Hold Rathna *Chikkamma's* hand and stay close to her at all times," she instructed her daughter. The school arranged a bus to take the children to Mysore, reaching the Palace by afternoon.

As she entered the vast Palace premises holding Rathna's hand, it felt like a dream to Kasthuri, and she couldn't believe her eyes. The grandeur of the royal Mysore Palace mesmerised her. Standing before the magnificent structure and witnessing its breathtaking beauty left her awestruck. "One could probably enter the heavens in the sky by climbing onto these towers," Kasthuri thought dreamily as she looked at the tall towers.

Rathna had to shake Kasthuri to bring her back to the present. The performing students and the accompanying teachers were accommodated within the Palace premises.

The grand Dashera festivities began the next day. An enormous stage was erected for the cultural show. As dusk settled, the Palace transformed into a radiant spectacle. The entire Palace was lit brilliantly with countless bulbs—a sight to behold!

It seemed to Kasthuri that the night sky was dotted with sparkling diamonds. "This can't be real! I surely must be dreaming!" an overwhelmed Kasthuri thought.

As a wave of immense joy engulfed her, Kasthuri danced with great energy and rhythm that evening alongside her group, and their performance received thunderous applause from the audience.

The next day, as they were about to leave for their respective destinations, they were informed that the *Maharaja* wanted to see all the children at the *Durbar* hall.

As Kasthuri entered the grand Durbar Hall, holding her aunt's hand, she felt overwhelmed at the sight of the king, who sat regally on his golden throne. He was adorned with a diamond-studded crown and looked majestic. His ministers sat in rows on either side of him.

The student-teacher group paid their respects to the king by bowing with folded hands. The *Durbar* assistant then guided each student forward one by one as the king presented a gift to each of them.

It was now Kasthuri's turn to walk up to the king, and she felt butterflies in her stomach as she was led to His Majesty. Kasthuri folded her hands respectfully in a traditional *Namaskara* as she approached the king. With an affectionate smile, the king handed Kasthuri a heavy, bright-green silk brocade bag.

Seeing the *Maharaja* of Mysore, Nalawadi Krisnaraja Wodeyar, lovingly called Rajarshi, from such close quarters and accepting a gift from him was nothing short of a beautiful dream for Kasthuri.

Once back on the bus, she curiously opened the silk bag to find a beautiful rectangular ivory jewellery box with intricate, colourful *meenakari* floral carvings. She held the box close to her chest; it would be her most prized possession.

The next day at school, Kasthuri spoke to her friend about nothing but the royal Palace and the benevolent *Maharaja.*

Chapter 7

Ramanuja had two young daughters, Radha and Manjula. Both girls were good-looking and good-natured as well. The couple performed the marriage of their older daughter, Radha, a couple of years back, with the son of industrialist Parthasarathy. The couple now sought a suitable alliance for their younger daughter, Manjula.

"When we have a fine boy in front of our eyes, why should we waste our time looking elsewhere?" Anasuya suggested.

"Who are you referring to, Anasuya?"

"I'm referring to our Narayana." Anasuya had grown quite fond of the young man. He had proven to be efficient and trustworthy, and she found him to be humble and respectful at all times.

"I agree! I wonder why I never thought of it. Nothing could give me more happiness than forging an alliance with my dear friend Keshava's family. Let's go to Sakleshpur tomorrow and speak to Alamelamma," Ramanuja said excitedly.

The couple set off for Sakleshpur the very next morning. After enjoying the piping-hot idlis and coconut chutney that

Alamelamma had served them, Ramanuja presented their proposal. Alamelamma could not believe her ears. Even in her dreams, she never thought that a man of Ramanuja's stature would offer his daughter's hand in marriage to her son; needless to say, she agreed happily. However, she expressed a concern.

"*Anna*, by God's grace, Pankaja and Jalaja are happily married and well settled. Kasthuri is now 14 years old and nearing marriageable age. I wish to perform Kasthuri's marriage before Narayana is married."

"I understand your concern, Alamelamma! I will help you find a suitable boy for Kasthuri. If all goes well, we could perform both weddings together," Ramanuja suggested, and Alamelamma happily nodded in agreement.

Alamelamma visited her parents' house in the evening and shared the good news. Although her parents were thrilled, Rathna seemed quiet. A puzzled Alamelamma asked her sister what the matter was.

"*Akka*! I am very happy for Narayana. But our Kasthuri is still young and doing very well at school. It is not fair or right to disturb her in the name of marriage."

"Rathna, it is important that Kasthuri gets married and settles down happily before her brother does, since I do not know what the future holds for me." Alamelamma tried to reason with an indifferent Rathna.

I am counting on you to convince and coax Kasthuri into marriage since she listens to you and no one else," Alamelamma pleaded, but Rathna remained unresponsive.

"Do not worry, Alamelu; I shall come in the evening and convince Kasthuri to marry," Kamalamma reassured her worried daughter.

As planned, Kamalamma came by the following evening. Alamelamma was sitting on the verandah, making garlands for the deities. Rathna and Kasthuri had just finished their dance practice and joined the two women. Sensing that the time was right, Kamalamma slowly broached the topic of marriage.

"Kasthuri! Ramanuja *Mama* has proposed his daughter, Manjula, in marriage to your brother. Though Amma has agreed to the proposal, she wishes to see you married before your brother gets married," Kamalamma said. Kasthuri, who was casually listening to her grandmother, was in for a rude shock.

"*Amma*, what is *Ajji* saying?" Kasthuri asked in disbelief.

"Kasthuri! I am growing old and wish to see you married before your brother is married."

"*Amma*, what is the connection between Narayana *Anna's* marriage and mine? Narayana *Anna's* marriage is fixed. So, please get him married."

"Kasthuri, you must understand your mother's concern for you. You need to be considerate, too. When your parents suggested marriage, didn't your sisters agree without saying a word? Look how happy they are now!" Kamalamma made her point.

"*Ajji*, Pankaja Akka, and Jalaja Akka were never interested in school and learning. It was their wish to be married. I do not share their interest in marriage. My only interest is to study well and become a graduate." Kasthuri answered.

"Kasthuri, you are 14 years old. Most girls of your age are either getting married or are already married. I wish to fulfil my responsibility before, God forbid, something were to happen to me. I cannot trust anyone with your responsibility, my dear! Hence the urgency. Is it too much to ask for?" Alamelamma became emotional.

"*Amma*, it was Appa's wish that I should study hard and graduate. He had mentioned it to you several times as well. How could you forget the dream that *Appa* and I shared? Did it never mean anything to you?" asked an agitated Kasthuri as she broke into tears.

At this point, Rathna, who had been listening calmly up to this moment, intervened. She gathered Kasthuri in her arms and consoled her, wiping away her tears.

"Hush, my darling, hush! Could you both please stop bothering the child? Do not force Kasthuri into something that is against her wishes. I shall not allow that." She warned her sister and mother.

She then turned to Kasthuri and said, "Kasthuri, do not cry, *Putta*! I shall ensure that nobody goes against your wishes." She slowly walked Kasthuri, who was still sobbing, to her room.

"What would I do without you, *Chikkamma?* No one understands me the way you do", Kasthuri said as she lovingly hugged her aunt.

"All will be fine, putta. You may go back to school as usual. Do not worry," Rathna assured Kasthuri, wiping away her tears. Kasthuri smiled through her tears.

When Rathna walked out onto the verandah, she saw Kamalamma and Alamelamma sitting with downcast faces, lost in their thoughts. Kamalamma was furious with her younger daughter for not supporting Alamelamma in this time of need.

"Rathna, I'm already extremely sad that you're not married. Do you want your sister to worry about Kasthuri as much as I worry about you? Do you want Kasthuri to stay unmarried, just like you, and listen to people's taunts?" Kamalamma asked. Her mother's words hurt Rathna. However, she immediately gathered herself to explain her intentions to her mother.

"*Amma*, I am not against Kasthuri getting married. All I am saying is that it is too early, and such haste would frighten the child. We could wait a couple more years to get her married. Kasthuri would then be old and mature enough to balance her marital responsibilities and studies."

Rathna then went to her sister, who was sobbing softly. She sat close to her, trying to console her. Alamelamma was visibly angry with Rathna for taking Kasthuri's side. "Rathna, I am disappointed in you," she said as she walked into the house in a huff.

Ramanuja was informed of Kasthuri's indifference to marriage. "It is not wise to force the Child into marriage at this point. Let us wait for a year or two. I shall look for the best boy for our Kasthuri," Ramanuja assured Alamelamma.

Narayana and Manjula were married shortly thereafter on an auspicious day in Mysore. The family returned to Sakleshpur with the newlyweds for the *Satyanarayana puja*. Narayana entered the house for the first time as a married man, holding his lovely wife Manjula's hand.

Kasthuri and Rathna warmly welcomed the new couple with a traditional *Aarti*. Kasthuri held her sister-in-law's hand, excitedly showing her each room in the house.

On being strictly instructed by his mother, Bhagwan exhibited excellent behaviour in front of Manjula.

"*Athige*, do not be taken in by his innocent behaviour. He is putting up an act in front of you. " Kasthuri teased her brother, and Bhagwan pinched his sister's hand before running away.

"Did you see what he just did, *Athige?* Didn't I tell you the boy is a brat?" Kasthuri proved her point, and Manjula laughed out loud.

Although Manjula missed her parents and home dearly, she felt overwhelmed by all the love and attention her new family showered upon her. She enjoyed her time at her new house in Sakleshpur and developed a special bond with the bubbly and lovely Kasthuri, who grew equally fond of her sister-in-law.

Manjula was an expert in hair styling and would style Kasthuri's hair differently each day. Kasthuri would rush to the mirror to admire herself with the latest hairstyle. She loved it so much that she would run back to her sister-in-law, hold her hands, and dance around, giggling happily. "Kasthuri, stop turning me round and round. I feel giddy." Manjula would lovingly complain.

"Narayana, why don't you go to Mysore and look for a suitable house for you both?" Alamelamma suggested after a month. Narayana soon found a suitable house and returned to Sakleshpur a few days later.

"*Amma*, I have found a small two-room house with all the facilities close to Ramanuja *Mama's* house and the coffee shop," he declared happily.

"In that case, you could take Manjula to Mysore and set up your new house together," she said. The young couple soon left for Mysore, their hearts filled with beautiful dreams about their future together.

Time flew by, and Kasthuri turned 15 years old. She passed her fourth form with flying colours, standing first in all subjects again. During the school assembly, her principal, Sir Albert Victor, congratulated and presented her with a large, shiny shield. While all the children cheered and clapped for Kasthuri, Bhagwan was the loudest. He was incredibly proud of his sister's achievement. Kasthuri was now promoted to the fifth form.

After school, Kasthuri and Bhagwan walked home joyfully, holding the shield. As they entered the gate of their house, Kasthuri recalled the day she brought a shield home to her proud father, and a tear rolled down her cheek.

Alamelamma was very happy when Kasthuri placed the shield in her hands. She planted a kiss on Kasthuri's cheek. "Kasthuri, quickly freshen up while I prepare your favourite potato *bondas* in a jiffy." Kasthuri excitedly ran towards the backyard wash area, followed by Bhagwan.

The next day, in math class, Sir Albert spoke about the annual school competitions scheduled for the following week. "Juliet! Kasthuri! I have never seen either of you participate in these competitions. I would want to understand why."

"Sir, most of these competitions are sports-based. We can't participate in those with our attire," Kasthuri promptly answered. The boys in the class suddenly burst out laughing. Kasthuri's face turned red with embarrassment. She hung her head, tears rolling down her cheeks.

"Quiet! Laughing at your classmates and ridiculing them is not right, and it's not funny," Sir Victor said, sounding angry. "I should have been more thoughtful," he thought to himself. "Kasthuri, do not cry, child! One shouldn't feel ashamed or sad because of the insensitive behaviour of a few others." Kasthuri wiped her tears and looked up at her teacher.

"I would like to see you and your friend Juliet participate in the elocution competition next week. The topic is *war and peace.*' Cheer up and prepare well."

Once home, an upset Kasthuri sat in her father's armchair on the verandah. So lost was she in her thoughts that her mother's repeated calls for her to freshen up and eat her snacks did not reach Kasthuri's ears. After receiving no response from Kasthuri, Alamelamma walked onto the verandah and found Kasthuri still in school attire, seeming annoyed. Upon seeing her mother, Kasthuri broke down.

"*Amma*, the boys in our class think we girls are good for nothing. They think our attire is funny and do not respect our feelings."

"Kasthuri, hasn't Rathna *Chikkamma* always told you not to place too much importance on what others think of you? It is what you think of yourself that counts."

"You are right, *Amma*! I feel we girls are better than those silly, disrespectful boys any time." She said as she got up and walked into the house.

With Rathna's help, Kasthuri prepared thoroughly for the elocution. Surprisingly, on the day of the competition, she felt no fear but a strong determination to prove to the boys in her class that girls could outperform them if they put their hearts into it. Kasthuri spoke effortlessly and powerfully on the topic, earning great appreciation from the judges.

As Sir Albert called out her name to collect the winner's prize, she walked onto the stage with her head held high, a sense of pride sweeping her. She made it a point to look at the audience as she accepted her prize, feeling happy and empowered.

Chapter 8

Narayana and Manjula had settled comfortably into their new house. They were extremely happy with their life together as husband and wife. Narayana was no longer a salaried employee at the flourishing coffee shop, having been made an equal partner by his father-in-law.

Now that he was earning well and was financially equipped to care for his family, he requested that his mother stop her small-scale business and rest at home, to which Alamelamma agreed without much resistance. She was now completely relaxed and had ample free time at her disposal.

A few months had passed, and Kasthuri noticed that her mother seemed to have lost weight and was starting to look pale. Also, Alamelamma had not been eating very well. A worried Kasthuri kept asking her mother what was wrong and if she felt okay. Alamelamma brushed aside the topic, stating that she was perfectly fine.

When Rathna came home in the evening, Kasthuri shared her concerns about her mother's well-being with her aunt. Rathna also agreed with Kasthuri that Alamelamma seemed to be looking frail. After considerable persuasion, Alamelamma consented to visit Doctor Rangachari. Following a thorough check-up and a few routine questions, he found no abnormalities in Alamelamma's physical health. He asked Alamelamma to sit outside while he wrote the prescription.

"She probably is worried about something, as a result of which she has lost her appetite and because of which she seems to be losing weight," he said to Kasthuri and Rathna, who looked at each other, puzzled at what the doctor had just said. Upon reaching home, a tired Alamelamma sat on the swing while Rathna and Kasthuri dragged a couple of chairs and sat close to her. Meanwhile, Kamalamma, who had just come by, joined them, too.

"*Akka,* Dr. Rangachari feels nothing is wrong with you physically. However, he believes you might be worried about something, which may be why you're not eating well," a concerned Rathna said.

"Didn't I repeatedly tell you that I am doing fine, despite which you both have forcefully taken me to the doctor! What a criminal waste of money!"

"*Amma,* is there something that worries you? Please tell us," Kasthuri urged. Alamelamma remained silent despite repeated pleas and coaxing.

"I think I know what must be bothering Alamelu. She seems to be worried about Kasthuri's wedding." Kasthuri and Rathna looked at Kamalamma in shock and surprise.

"*Amma,* is it true that you are worried about my marriage?" Kasthuri asked. Alamelamma did not reply but looked down, beginning to scratch the wooden plank of the swing with the nail of her index finger.

"I am sure that is what is bothering her. She is probably hesitating to bring it up since you both would not listen to her anyway. I am her mother, and I understand my daughter's thoughts," Kamalamma said.

At this point, Alamelamma broke down and started to cry. After a while, she regained her composure and began to speak.

"Rathna, I have been worried about Kasthuri's wedding since the passing of my husband," she said. "If God forbade something were to happen to me tomorrow, and I too leave the world just as suddenly as my husband did, who would care for my Kasthuri?"

"*Amma*, nothing will happen to you. Moreover, my siblings and, most importantly, Rathna Chikkamma are here to care for you and me, too, if needed." Kasthuri tried to reassure her mother.

"Getting you married is my responsibility. I do not want to burden anyone, be it your aunt, sisters, or brother."

A long lull of calm and silence prevailed as the four women were lost in their thoughts. "*Amma!*" Kasthuri's voice tore through the difficult silence. "*Amma*, if getting me married would make you feel at peace, so be it."

"Kasthuri! My darling! Did I hear you right?" Alamelamma sounded unbelievably happy.

"Yes! However, I have a condition. I would only agree to marry Someone who values education and would not object to my zeal to pursue education after marriage." Kasthuri was firm.

"I promise you, my darling, that we will find a wonderful boy for you who will not only love you but also support and encourage you in pursuing your education," Alamelamma gave her word. Her happiness knew no bounds.

Kasthuri nodded and slowly walked toward her room. Contrary to her sister's happiness, Rathna felt helpless and sad as Kasthuri quietly walked into the house. She followed her niece into her room and sat down to speak to her. "Kasthuri, *Putta*! forgive me for failing to stand by you this time," Rathna said in a choked voice as extreme guilt swept over her.

"Please do not feel bad, *Chikkamma*. In the given situation and with Amma's well-being being our priority, I understand that you might have felt as helpless as I have to say anything against *Amma's* wish".

"Kasthuri, are you aware that Kadambani joined college and pursued her medical degree after getting married? Her husband and in-laws encouraged her to achieve her dream. So, do not worry. It is possible to study equally well after marriage." Rathna tried hard to keep up Kasthuri's spirit while Kasthuri nodded.

Alamelamma informed Ramanuja that Kasthuri had finally consented to marry and shared with him the condition she had put forth. Ramanuja assured her he would find a suitable boy just right for Kasthuri.

Unfortunately, even though many boys liked Kasthuri's photograph and the horoscopes matched, neither the boys nor their families favoured allowing Kasthuri to pursue further studies. Just as Alamelamma was about to lose hope of finding a suitable boy for her daughter, Ramanuja arrived in Sakleshpur unannounced on a Sunday with a photograph and horoscope of a prospective groom.

"A well-educated boy from a wealthy Telugu *Srivaishnavite* family is seeking a suitable bride. They reside in Tadipatri, a town in the Anantapur district," Ramanuja explained happily.

"The prospective groom, Srinivasa, is a graduate in mathematics and works as a manager at a reputed private firm in the same town. The family liked Kasthuri's photograph, and the horoscopes matched, too. Most importantly, they favoured Kasthuri to continue her education after the marriage," Ramanuja continued enthusiastically.

Alamelamma and her parents were extremely happy. However, they had some concerns. One was that the boy's family was a Telugu-speaking Srivaishnavite family from Andhra Pradesh. Kasthuri neither understood nor spoke a word of Telugu.

The other concern was the distance between the groom's town and Sakleshpur. However, after extensive discussions throughout the day and weighing all the pros and cons, everyone agreed it would be wise to proceed with this alliance.

Rathna and Alamelamma sat down with Kasthuri that night. They informed her about the prospective groom, his family, and the decision to go ahead with the alliance.

Kasthuri had only one question: "*Chikkamma*, will I be able to continue my studies after marriage?"

"Yes, *Putta,* they have assured us that you can study as much as you wish," Rathna answered confidently.

In a week, the prospective groom, Srinivasa's older brother Venkatachary, and his wife, Lakshmamma, arrived at the Iyengar home in Sakleshpur. Venkatachary, a double graduate who worked as a headmaster in Tadipatri, was quite fluent in Tamil; therefore, the conversation was conducted in Tamil. Although Lakshmamma barely understood the language, she politely sat through the entire discussion.

The couple took an instant liking to the lovely Kasthuri, and the customary *Vathle Pak* was exchanged between the families of Kasthuri and Srinivasa Chary. Since Kasthuri's fifth-form final exams were scheduled to commence in a month's time, an auspicious *Muhurtham* was fixed for the marriage of Kasthuri and Srinivasa to be held two weeks after her exams.

The following day, Kasthuri went to school with her brother as usual. Her dear friend Juliet stood at the door waiting for her with a smile. Unlike on other days, Kasthuri appeared dull and sad.

"Kasthuri! What is the matter? You look so pale!"

"Julie, *Amma* is marrying me to a Telugu-speaking boy and sending me away to a distant place. I will not be able to see you after the exams," Kasthuri said, tears welling up in her eyes. The unexpected news shocked Juliet, making it hard for her to fathom that she wouldn't be able to see Kasthuri after the exams. The two friends felt sad and dejected throughout the day.

Back home, the Iyengar family received the joyful news that Jalaja would return to Bangalore with her children and, a week later, travel to Sakleshpur. Alamelamma was ecstatic that Jalaja was coming home just before Kasthuri's wedding.

As they were all chatting happily that evening, they heard the sounds of a horse cart stopping at the gate. Sir Albert Victor, Kasthuri's math teacher and school principal, walked in, taking everyone by surprise. A delighted Kasthuri ran out to welcome her teacher with joy. Alamelamma and the others stood up with folded hands out of respect and offered him a chair to sit in.

"Alamelamma, I have heard from Juliet's father that arrangements are being made to get Kasthuri married and sent away. I'm sorry, but the news has upset me," Sir Albert said.

"Yes, respected Sir! Kasthuri's marriage to a nice boy has been arranged, and we plan to hold the wedding in a month."

"Kasthuri is an extraordinary student and a prodigy. She could do wonders and bring us laurels if allowed to continue her education uninterrupted. Therefore, with folded hands, I humbly request that you kindly cancel this wedding and enable the Child to study happily." Sir Victor concluded.

"Sir, my daughter is fortunate to have a great teacher and well-wisher like you. However, I wish to perform Kasthuri's marriage while I am still healthy."

"What about Kasthuri's wish to study?" questioned Sir Albert.

"I assure you, Sir, that we have, with the utmost care, ensured that Kasthuri is wedded into an education-oriented family that would wholeheartedly support her future education."

Sir Albert nodded. He had Kasthuri sit beside him and engage in a brief conversation: "Kasthuri, you have been and will forever be my favourite student. Come what may, remember never to give up on your dreams, my child!"

Sir Victor took leave of everyone and left. Kasthuri walked him to the gate to see him off. Sir Victor climbed onto his cart and looked at Kasthuri as the cart moved. The sight of Kasthuri waving to him innocently made his heart heavy. "May the Lord be with you, my child"! He softly muttered as the horses galloped ahead.

Chapter 9

It was a joyous day at the Iyengar household. While Narayana and Manjula arrived in Sakleshpur the previous night, Pankaja and Jalaja's families came just in time for breakfast. Alamelamma's joy knew no bounds; she felt ecstatic to have all her children and grandchildren in the house.

Govind and Jalaja's adorable twin children, Abhiram and Anandi, became the centre of everyone's attention. Despite her exams being just around the corner, Kasthuri managed to steal time to play with her little nephews and niece.

Alamelamma was determined to conduct her youngest daughter's wedding well and to the best of her ability. Although Venkatachary's family firmly refused to accept dowry or anything else, she decided to give Kasthuri the jewellery she had lovingly prepared for her over the years, along with the customary silver puja items.

The wedding festivities were in full swing. Invitation cards were printed and sent to all the near and dear ones.

The same choultry where the marriages of Pankaja and Jalaja were performed had been booked for the three-day wedding. A guest house had been reserved for the 25-member groom party.

Cook Madhavan and his team, who had done an excellent job at older girls' weddings, were roped in yet again to serve delicacies for Kasthuri's wedding, too. Although the groom's family did not interfere in deciding the wedding menu, Alamelamma felt it would also be nice to include a few Andhra dishes.

"Madhavan *Anna*, as you know, Kasthuri's groom and his family hail from Andhra. Can we serve a few Andhra items at lunch on the wedding day?"

"Sure, Alamelamma! We could have a mixed wedding lunch menu, a combination of Andhra and Karnataka cuisine."

The guests arrived one by one, and the three sisters of Keshavamurthy, along with their husbands, were the first ones to arrive.

"Alamelamma, why did you choose a boy from a faraway Andhra? Couldn't we have found a suitable boy in Karnataka itself for our lovely girl?" the husband of Ahalya, the oldest sister-in-law, inquired after a leisurely lunch.

"*Anna*, we have found several good matches from equally good families for Kasthuri. Although they were all very interested in marrying Kasthuri, none of them were willing to support Kasthuri in her future educational endeavours, which was Kasthuri's only condition for marriage."

"How about this boy and his family?"

"The boy, Srinivasa, and his family are not only highly educated but also willing to wholeheartedly support Kasthuri in continuing her education after marriage."

"Strange are the ways of God, and no one or nothing can change His plan. It has been destined that Kasthuri should marry and spend the rest of her life in Andhra," he remarked philosophically.

It was the day of Kasthuri's last exam and her final day at the Hardwicke Mission School, which had been her second home for the past few years. The thought of not being able to set foot on this school campus again pained her. Tears began to roll down her cheeks as she stood at the gate, gazing at her school with affection.

A worried Bhagwan shook his sister and asked her why she was crying. She brushed him off and walked toward her classroom, wiping her tears. Bhagwan stood there watching his sister, and seeing her so sad, broke his heart.

As usual, her dear friend Juliet stood at the classroom door, smiling and waiting for her. Kasthuri ran to hug her friend and cried her heart out.

"Julie, today is my last day at school. I won't be able to see this school again, and I won't be able to see you again," Kasthuri started to cry.

Kasthuri's words also cause Juliet to break down. As she wiped her tears, Juliet tried to console Kasthuri too. "Do not cry, Kasthuri! God willing, we could meet sometime when you come down to Sakleshpur with your family," said Juliet hopefully.

Unlike every other exam, where she would usually be the first to finish, for some reason, this time, Kasthuri found it very difficult to write her exam quickly, despite knowing all the answers. The pen wouldn't move as fast as it should have. After 15 minutes of grace time that teacher Andrew kindly granted her, she finished writing her last exam.

"What is the matter, Kasthuri? Aren't you feeling well?" Teacher Andrew sounded concerned.

"Nothing at all, Sir! I am doing well. Thank you"

Kasthuri excused herself and walked toward Sir Albert's room to take his leave and bid him farewell. Sir Albert was reviewing files scattered across his desk when Kasthuri knocked on his door. Sir Albert looked up through his silver-plated, round-rimmed spectacles to see her standing at the entrance.

"Kasthuri! There you are! Come on in, Child! I hope you wrote your exam well, as always!"

"Yes, Sir! The exam went on pretty well. Today is my last day at school. I have come to see you and seek your blessings before I leave."

"Oh yes, Kasthuri! I thought about it yesterday, but it slipped my mind today. I am sorry! Old age is catching up with me, I guess," he laughed as he got up from his chair and walked over to Kasthuri.

"May the Lord's grace always shine upon you, sweet child!" he said, lovingly touching her head.

" Oh, wait, Kasthuri!" Sir Albert said to Kasthuri as she turned back to leave. He approached his desk and picked up the beautiful Conway Stewart pen on his table. "Here, Kasthuri! I am sure you will remember this old teacher of yours whenever you see this pen," Sir Albert said, smiling as he handed her the pen.

"How could I ever forget you, Sir?" Kasthuri accepted the gift and folded her hands in a respectful gesture.

With his flowing white robe, long white beard, long silvery hair, and affectionate smile, Kasthuri always regarded Sir Albert as a grandfather figure. His gentle demeanour and polite conversational ways endeared him to all the children, including Kasthuri. The fact that he taught her favourite subject enhanced her respect for him.

"May the passion for learning shine brightly within you always! Remember, Child! The day you stop learning, you will stop growing!" he advised before Kasthuri left.

She then bid a heartfelt goodbye to her dear friend Juliet and walked to the school gate, surprised to see her brother waiting for her.

"What brings you to the gate so early, Bhagwan? Have your friends not come to school today?" asked Kasthuri.

"*Akka*, I realised today is the last day I'll be walking back home with you. Hence, I rushed to the gate as soon as the bell struck," an unusually emotional Bhagwan said with tears in his eyes. His words touched Kasthuri; she felt immense love for her little brother.

"Don't cry, Bhagwan," Kasthuri said, but she couldn't control her own tears as she wiped her brother's tears with the edge of her sari. The two of them slowly began to walk back home, their hearts heavy, holding each other's hands in complete silence. Words somehow failed the otherwise talkative duo that afternoon.

Chapter 10

With only a week left until Kasthuri's wedding, other relatives and guests began to arrive, and the house was soon brimming with people. The hustle and bustle, the appetising aroma from the kitchen, the sounds of happy conversations and laughter, and the children giggling and playing around all added vibrancy and joy to the wedding house.

Three days before the wedding, the groom and his family also reached Sakleshpur by train. As soon as they alighted from the train, the bride's family respectfully welcomed them with floral garlands.

Srinivasa Chary was a dark, handsome man of medium height. He wore a pure white dhoti and a shirt, over which he donned a navy blue coat. He tied his hair into a bun and wore a turban to cover his head. Diamonds sparkled in each of his earlobes. A traditional namam on his forehead made his face look brighter.

As he alighted from the train, Srinivasa greeted the bride's family with folded hands and a gentle smile. He was a picture of grace and respectability. Upon seeing the groom, Narayana felt happy and reassured for his little sister.

After exchanging pleasantries, the groom and his family were gently ushered to the horse carts waiting outside the railway station to take them to the guest house where they had been arranged to stay.

That evening, after the *Daivaradhane* puja at home, Kasthuri and her family left for the choultry. The groom and his family arrived shortly thereafter. They were warmly welcomed by the bride's family with fresh, fragrant lily garlands and were led in, accompanied by the traditional *Nadaswaram* tunes played by expert musicians.

From this point on, the priest took over. With the bride and groom's families on either side, the priest instructed the bride and groom to step toward each other one step at a time for the *Varamala* ritual. Narayana handed the bride and groom beautiful garlands made of lovely pink roses.

Kasthuri looked resplendent in a light pink *Kanjeevaram* saree adorned with a bright golden border and peacock motifs. The diamond jewellery she wore shone brightly in the evening light. She looked like a beautiful goddess standing there, her hands holding a garland of flowers.

A fun competition of sorts had now begun. The groom's family demanded that the bride take the first step, while the bride's family insisted that the groom take the first step. Finally, as the bride and the groom walked closer, Kasthuri was asked to garland her groom. Kasthuri looked up at him and saw him smiling gently while she garlanded him. Kasthuri experienced a strange sense of reassurance in his presence.

When the groom was about to garland Kasthuri, Narayana and Kasthuri's uncles lifted her high to tease him. Not ones to concede defeat, the groom's brothers and cousins lifted him even higher, and Srinivasa Chary succeeded in garlanding his lovely bride. Amidst the fun, laughter, and playful teasing, the *Varamala* ritual concluded on a joyful note.

The weather was pleasant the next morning, the day of Kasthuri's wedding. The wedding hall was beautifully decorated with freshly bloomed roses, marigolds, lilies, jasmine, and multicoloured dahlias. Tall green banana stems, mango leaves, and flowers made from coconut leaves were arranged at the entrance and around the mandapa, enhancing the traditional look of the venue. A beautifully decorated board displaying the names of the bride and groom was placed at the entrance of the choultry.

The groom's family, dressed in their finest silks and brocades, was led toward the tastefully decorated *mandapam,* where the wedding rituals would be performed. Srinivasa, attired in a fine, pure silk *dhoti* with golden borders and a matching *uttareeyam* draping his chest, presented a picture of dignity and grace.

Guests started arriving at the venue one by one. The musicians playing the *Nadaswaram, Mridangam,* and *Ghatam* enthusiastically performed classical *Krithis* and other melodies. The divine music, the fragrance of fresh lilies and jasmine, the heavenly aroma from the burning incense, and the priests chanting Vedic hymns all created the perfect atmosphere for a beautiful wedding.

Kasthuri, dressed in a 9-yard red *Kanjeevaram* saree with a golden border tied in the madisaar fashion and with her hair styled in an Andal kondai, looked like the beautiful Iyengar bride she was. The heavy gold temple-style jewellery she wore added to her regal look. A bright red *namam* adorned her forehead, replacing the usual red round *bindi* she usually kept.

In her father's absence, it was decided that her brother Narayana and his wife Manjula would perform the *Kanyadaanam* ritual, where the bride is given to the groom.

Kasthuri recalled the *Kanyadaanam* ritual of her two older sisters when their father gave them to their grooms while they sat on his lap. She missed her father more than ever, and a tear fell from her eye as she sat on her brother's lap for the ritual.

The *Mangalya Dharanam* and the *Saptapadi* rituals were completed, and little Kasthuri was now a married woman. Srinivasa and Kasthuri were now husband and wife. Kasthuri felt a wave of shyness and awkwardness sweep over her as she sat beside her husband. However, the gentleman that he was, Srinivasa, tried to make Kasthuri feel at ease with his subtle, tender gestures and dignified behaviour.

The wedding lunch was a grand and elaborate affair, featuring a vast spread served traditionally on freshly cut plantain leaves. As the cooks served one delicious item after another on the glossy leaves, the groom and his family were pleasantly surprised and delighted by the inclusion of the tangy Tomato *Pappu*, the wholesome *Gutti Vankaya*, and the spicy *Mirapakaya bajji* on the menu, along with the typical

Karnataka Iyengar style wedding spread that included *Obbattu, Paayasa, Ambode, Puliyogare,* Potato fry, Beans *palya, Sambar, Rasam,* curds, and pickle. Cook Madhavan and his team did a fantastic job once again.

Kasthuri was set to leave for Anantapur with the groom and his family the following day. Alamelamma, Rathna, and Kasthuri's maternal aunts and uncles would also accompany them. With bags packed, it was time to head to the railway station. The cooks had neatly packed *Uppittu* and *Akki Rotti* in brass containers to be enjoyed on the train, along with large boxes of wedding sweets.

The train arrived at the platform, and the luggage was swiftly loaded. Kasthuri bid an emotional farewell to her siblings, who had come to see her off, and boarded the train with the others. "Kasthuri, you could sit on that seat next to your husband," Alamelamma said. As Kasthuri hesitantly walked to her seat, her husband looked up at her and smiled gently.

"Would you want to sit by the window, Kasthuri?" Srinivasa asked in English as he spoke to his wife for the first time. Kasthuri nodded in the affirmative. Srinivasa graciously vacated his window seat for his wife and took the seat next to her.

Kasthuri looked out the window and waved to her siblings, tears blurring her vision. At that moment, Bhagwan, who had been holding back his tears all along, began to cry inconsolably. In an instant, Kasthuri sprang up, ran out of the compartment, and pulled her little brother into an emotional embrace. Srinivasa, too, followed her and stood there calmly.

"*Akka*! Do not leave!" Bhagwan said as he sobbed. Srinivasa's heart went out to the little boy.

"Do not cry, Bhagwan! You may visit Anantapur whenever you wish to see your sister, and I shall bring Kasthuri to Sakleshpur whenever she wishes to see you. Would that be alright?" Srinivasa asked with a smile.

Srinivasa's reassuring words touched Bhagwan's little heart, and he hugged his brother-in-law tightly amidst tears. Although Bhagwan's sudden gesture initially took Srinivasa aback, he wrapped his arms around the boy and patted his back soothingly. The loud sound of the train horn created a sense of urgency, prompting Srinivasa to gently guide his wife back onto the train.

The train arrived at Tadipatri station around 9 p.m. During the day, numerous horse carts, referred to by the local people as *Jatka*, could easily be found outside the station. However, finding one at a late hour was challenging, as the cartmen needed to be informed in advance if their services were required at night.

"Srinivasa, have you instructed Veera to inform the cartmen to pick us all up outside the station tonight?"

"Yes, Anna. Veera would do the needful. Not to worry." As expected, around half a dozen *jatkas* were waiting outside the railway station to pick them up.

The house was about a kilometre away from the station. The streets were pitch dark, empty, and eerily silent. The town dwellers were early risers and went to bed very early, too, and hence, not a single soul was seen on the streets.

The absolute silence made the sounds of galloping horses feel extremely loud to the ears. A couple of lanterns hung at the front of each *jatka*, guiding the horses along the way. A few strays barked in the distance, and an owl hooted incessantly. Kasthuri held on tightly to her aunt as they made their way home.

"Bhadra! Veera!" Srinivasa called out loudly to the men servants to open the gates.

"*Ayya! vasthunnaa!* (Sir, I'm coming)," Bhadra answered as he ran to open the gate with a lantern in his hand. Veera, too, followed him, carrying a couple of huge lanterns.

The cartmen brought the luggage down, handed it to Bhadra, and left after collecting their fare. As Bhadra and Veera held up the lanterns to show the way to the house, everyone else followed them.

There were giant trees all around, the dry leaves of which kept falling on the ground, making a crackling sound as they walked ahead one by one. It was quite a distance from the gate to the house. The sounds of occasional mooing were heard as they walked past the *cow shed*.

"*Chikkamma*, how far are we going to walk like this? There are only trees everywhere. I don't see the house," Kasthuri remarked.

"Look right in front, Kasthuri! There! Can you see the light?" Rathna asked as she pointed toward the house.

Lakshmi's parents warmly welcomed the newlywed couple and the other guests into the house with a traditional *aarti*.

Kasthuri was asked to hold her husband's hand and step forward with her right foot as she entered her marital home for the first time. "This is your house, Kasthuri! Our house!" Srinivasa whispered to Kasthuri lovingly. Kasthuri suddenly felt shy and glanced downward.

The wedding rituals and travel had worn everyone out. Soon after bathing and having dinner, everyone collapsed into the comfort of their beds.

Kasthuri was awakened by the warm, early morning sun rays that touched her face. She pulled the cotton blanket over her head and curled up lazily. The crowing of roosters and the mooing of cows grew louder, disturbing the morning silence and Kasthuri's slumber. Reluctantly, she sat up in bed, rubbing her eyes as she looked around to find the room empty. Her mother and aunts, who shared the room, were nowhere to be seen. She got up immediately, walked out, and saw them helping Lakshmi in the kitchen. At the same time, Rathna entered the living room from the backyard after her bath.

"Kasthuri! There you are! I was just about to wake you up! "Rathna said as she walked up to Kasthuri.

"I have kept your clothes and toiletries on the window ledge in the washroom. Would you hurry up and take your bath now?" Rathna urged Kasthuri.

As she rushed toward the backyard, Kasthuri bumped hard into her husband, who was coming out of his room, fully dressed to go to work. The turban on his head fell to the floor. "I am sorry! I should have been more careful!" said a concerned Kasthuri.

"It wasn't your mistake, Kasthuri. I rushed out of the room pretty fast, too. Hope you're not hurt!" he said to her as he bent down to pick up his turban. Kasthuri liked his sensitivity and concern for her.

After breakfast, the elders sat chatting leisurely in the spacious living area. "We are planning to have a small puja tomorrow to mark the new bride's arrival," Venkatachary announced.

"Also, since the newlywed couple's *nuptial night* has not been formally conducted so far, the priest has advised that there is an excellent muhurtham at 7 pm tomorrow to proceed with the ritual," he added, to which the bride's family agreed.

In the meantime, Kasthuri walked around the massive hallway of the *Manduva Logili* house, which was also an open, central courtyard home, similar to their *Thotti Mane* at Sakleshpur but much larger and more spacious. While Kasthuri continued to explore the palatial house, Rathna called her, "Kasthuri! Lakshmi *Akka* wants to show us your room! Come along!"

Kasthuri joined them as Lakshmi led them into a spacious, well-ventilated room decorated with beautifully carved rosewood furniture. The room featured a four-poster bed and a large wooden almirah embossed with a picture of the goddess Lakshmi seated on a lotus, with coins raining down from her right palm. A pair of wicker chairs was placed by the window alongside a finely polished rosewood table with intricate carvings.

"Srinivasa hired the best craftsman in town to prepare the furniture for this room. He specifically had that table done for Kasthuri so she could comfortably keep her books on it and study," Lakshmi explained

Kasthuri's eyes immediately turned to the table and chair. She visualised herself sitting in the chair, deeply engaged in study with books spread out on the table, as a fresh breeze from the window occasionally brushed her face. The thought made Kasthuri happy.

The puja was well attended by relatives and friends the next day. "Srinivasa surely must have offered prayers to the Lord with golden flowers in his past life to have been bestowed with such a beautiful wife in this life," Srinivasa's uncle remarked, while the others concurred.

Kasthuri and Srinivasa began their new life together as husband and wife in every sense from that night onward.

Chapter 11

It had been almost a fortnight since Kasthuri had moved into her new house, and her family planned to return to Sakleshpur shortly.

"Srinivasa, since your mother-in-law and others will be leaving for Sakleshpur in a couple of days, why don't you show them our farms?" Venkatachary suggested.

The following morning, Srinivasa took Kasthuri's family on a tour of their vast farmlands, which included beautiful mangroves, coconut farms, and lush green paddy fields. Needless to say, they were all pleased to see the prosperity of Kasthuri's marital home. Srinivasa instructed his farmhands to harvest and pack the finest mangoes and sweet limes for Kasthuri's family to take to Sakleshpur.

Soon, it was time for them to return to Sakleshpur. Kasthuri had never been away from her mother and aunt for more than a few days. The thought of living in this house alone, without her family around, made her feel sad.

"*Amma*, don't leave me and go," Kasthuri pleaded with her mother.

"With the love and support of your husband, you will do just fine, Kasthuri! Do not worry! Try learning Telugu as quickly as possible to converse with your sister-in-law comfortably." Kasthuri nodded as Alamelamma continued giving her instructions. "Also, though your sister-in-law seems too nice to ask for help, do take the initiative to assist her with household chores, and yes, eat well on time and practice your music regularly."

Kasthuri nodded as she approached Rathna and sat beside her while she packed her bag.

"Don't go, *chikkamma*," Kasthuri said with tears in her eyes. Rathna pulled her niece into a tight embrace and kissed her cheek.

"*Putta*, I'm leaving only after being completely reassured that my precious Kasthuri is safe. I am sure you would be happy in this house," Rathna reassured Kasthuri. However, Kasthuri continued to cry.

"I want to leave with a picture of my Kasthuri, happy and smiling. Please don't send me off with a sad face, my darling!"

"*Chikkamma*, what would I do without you?" Kasthuri started to cry.

"*Putta*, I will still be here whenever you need me. Your husband is a good man. Build a beautiful life with him," Rathna said.

"We are leaving the apple of our eyes here with you. Please take care of her as you would take care of your child," an emotional Alamelamma said to Venkatachary and Lakshmi, who lovingly reassured her.

Jatkas had been arranged to take them all to the railway station, and Kasthuri kept waving to her family as tears blurred her vision. As she stood at the gate, crying, Srinivasa consoled her and gently walked her in.

It had been about a month and a half since Kasthuri moved into her new home. Although she greatly missed her parental home and school, Kasthuri gradually adapted to her new surroundings and family.

Though Srinivasa was a man of few words, he left no stone unturned to make Kasthuri feel loved and cared for. Srinivasa was a disciplined yoga practitioner who never missed his early morning *yogabhyasa* and *dhyana*. A mathematics graduate, he worked as a *Dewan* at Krishna Swamy's estate while also managing the vast farms owned by his family.

Kasthuri's older brother-in-law, Venkatachary, was an exceptionally affectionate and soft-spoken man who, like his younger brother, was also an early riser. He held double degrees in History and English Literature and taught both subjects at the Zilla Parishad School in the town, where he served as the headmaster.

Venkatachary's wife, Lakshmi, was also soft-spoken, accommodating, and an excellent homemaker.

The couple's elder daughter was married and lived with her family, while the younger children, Aruna, Padmini, and Jagannath, were still in school.

Kasthuri slowly started to like her stay in her new house with her new family, thanks to the love and affection they all showered on her. While she conversed with Venkatachary in Tamil, she spoke English with Srinivasa and the children. She made it a point to learn a few words of Telugu each day and tried to converse with Lakshmi in the little Telugu she had learned.

That morning, Kasthuri was at the cowshed watching their house help, Manemma, skillfully milking the cows when she was distracted by Srinivasa's voice.

Srinivasa called out loudly from their room, "Kasthuri! Help me find my turban, will you?"

As she walked into the room, she found her husband in front of the mirror, adjusting his shirt while the turban lay on the cot. She wondered why her husband couldn't see the turban when it was right in front of him. Kasthuri picked up the turban and looked at him with a puzzled expression.

"Asking for the turban was an excuse to bring you back to me, Kasthuri! You seem to have gotten busy with everything and everyone except this poor husband of yours," he complained dramatically.

Kasthuri laughed at her husband's childlike attention-seeking gimmick as she approached him. She placed the turban on his head and wrapped her arms around his neck. Srinivasa generally came across as a poised man with a respectable demeanour. But when he was with Kasthuri, he was his true self, naughty and childlike.

"Who would believe that you could be such a child?" Kasthuri remarked teasingly.

Srinivasa hugged his dear wife tightly and kissed her cheek. "Kasthuri, a new movie produced by Swamy Garu's Vaarahi Studios, is in the town theatre. Swamy Garu has given me two balcony tickets to tomorrow evening's show for both of us. Would you like to go?"

"I would love to! I have never been to a theatre, let alone watch a movie!" Kasthuri said excitedly.

"I have never been to a theatre either, Kasthuri, and I'm equally excited for our first outing together—just the two of us!" Srinivasa said with a glint of mischief in his eyes.

"Aren't you getting late for work, your highness? Swamy *Garu* might come home looking for his trusted Dewan if you delay any longer. So, hurry, will you?"

"Only if you promise not to be out of my sight until I leave for work every morning!" Srinivasa put forth his condition. Kasthuri nodded and smiled as she fondly watched her husband leave for work, albeit reluctantly.

Srinivasa worked as a Dewan at Krishna Swamy's estate. Krishna Swamy owned several businesses and was also the founder of Varaahi Studios, the second largest in Asia at the time. He commanded a vast business empire and immense wealth. Krishna Swamy's estate was a sprawling 20-acre property where he and his family lived in a palatial house. The estate also housed various administrative offices for textiles, banking, oil mills, arrack contracting, and ceramics.

Krishna Swamy was extremely fond of the bright, sincere, hardworking Srinivasa. Such was his trust in Srinivasa that he entrusted him with the keys to his massive personal safety vaults, which contained documents of his properties and businesses, family gold and silver jewellery, and large amounts of cash. Srinivasa carried the keys with him even when he went home and handled them with the utmost responsibility.

The movie outing that evening with her husband was magical. Although Kasthuri didn't understand the Telugu movie well, the entire experience of watching the film on a massive screen while sitting in a plush, cushioned chair, holding her husband's hand, and listening to him whisper sweet nothings into her ear made her heart flutter. The cool air from the air coolers added to the pure bliss that Kasthuri cherished.

A week had passed. "Kasthuri! Krishna Swamy *Garu* has invited us to his house this evening. His mother and wife are eager to meet you! I will be home by 5 pm. Would you be ready by then?" he asked enthusiastically, to which Kasthuri nodded half-heartedly.

"What is the matter, Kasthuri?"

"I don't know anyone there, nor do I know their language. I feel slightly nervous."

"Swamy *Garu* and his family are extremely nice people, Kasthuri! I'm sure you will like them too." Srinivasa reassured.

As expected, Krishna Swamy's family welcomed Srinivasa and Kasthuri with open arms. Krishna Swamy's mother and wife immediately took a liking to the lovely Kasthuri. Swamy's wife handed Kasthuri a red velvet box. "Our wedding gift to you, Kasthuri," she said and requested that Kasthuri open the box.

Kasthuri and Srinivasa were pleasantly surprised to discover a grand emerald and pearl necklace in the box. Krishna Swamy's mother assisted Kasthuri in wearing the necklace and looked at her approvingly. A couple of hours later, they returned home after profusely thanking Swamy Garu and his family for their hospitality.

"Srinivasa, the schools will reopen in a week after the summer vacation, and we need to consider enrolling Kasthuri in a good school for her Matriculation," Venkatachary reminded his brother that evening during dinner.

"Instead of looking elsewhere, why not enrol Kasthuri in your school, Anna? With you and other highly knowledgeable teachers guiding her well, what more could one ask for?"

"Very well, then! You can bring Kasthuri to school tomorrow morning and finish all the admission formalities."

Chapter 12

That night after dinner, as Srinivasa walked into his room, he saw Kasthuri sitting by the window, gazing dreamily at the sky while humming a tune. A bright smile graced her face.

"Well! Well! Someone seems to be happy at the mention of school!" Srinivasa teased his wife.

Kasthuri turned to see Srinivasa standing at the door, smiling at her. She approached her husband and playfully pulled him into the room. She then danced around joyously, holding his hands.

"*Ree*, I'm thrilled. What time do we go to school tomorrow?" she asked excitedly.

"As soon as it opens," Srinivasa answered animatedly as Kasthuri's excitement caught on to him.

The following day, the couple visited the school. Srinivasa deposited 15 rupees in fees, thus formally enrolling Kasthuri in the Matriculation course at Zilla Parishad High School in Tadipatri. Kasthuri's joy knew no bounds.

That evening, when he got home, Venkatachary brought in a large, heavy bag and placed it on the wooden table in the living area. He sat down in a chair, wiped the sweat from his forehead, and drank a large glass of cool buttermilk handed to him by his wife.

"Where is Kasthuri?" he asked Lakshmi.

"She is in the kitchen preparing dinner," Lakshmi answered.

"Lakshmi, Kasthuri has been in the house for only a month and a half. Please do not burden her with responsibilities yet."

"I understand, but Kasthuri insisted on preparing dinner today," she replied.

"Padmini, please run into the kitchen and bring your aunt along?" Venkatachary said to Padmini, who was playing around. Shortly after, Kasthuri came into the living room, accompanied by Padmini.

"Kasthuri! I have brought all the textbooks for your matriculation. The school will start in a couple of weeks; until then, you can go through them during your free time".

Kasthuri nodded and beamed happily as she walked to her room, holding the books. She placed the bag on her table and gently took out the books. When her eyes fell on the math textbook, her heart skipped a beat, and she held the book lovingly close to her chest.

Srinivasa usually woke up even before the clock struck 5 for his Yogabhyasa and was always the first one awake in the house. Though he took care not to wake his wife, she would immediately wake up along with him.

"Kasthuri, the Sun hasn't risen yet. You do not have to wake up this early, my darling! Why don't you sleep for a little longer?" he would say lovingly. That morning, too, Srinivasa insisted that Kasthuri sleep a little longer.

"That's fine, *Ree.* I like waking up early, too. I shall bathe and go through the textbooks," she said as she opened the wooden almirah for a fresh set of clothes.

"*Aha*! Doesn't the table look nice now?" Srinivasa remarked as he entered the room, only to find his wife neatly arranging the books on the table. He approached her, gently took her by the shoulders, and helped her into the chair by the table. Stepping back, he looked on with contentment.

"Exactly how I had pictured!" He said happily. Kasthuri looked at her husband fondly. His childlike happiness made her happy as well. Her love and respect for her husband increased by the day.

A month passed. Kasthuri could now converse with Lakshmi in a mix of Telugu and Kannada, which Lakshmi thankfully understood.

"Srinivasa, it is mandatory for all newlywed couples in our family to visit Tirupati and seek the blessings of the Lord. It would be nice if both of you could make a short visit before Kasthuri gets busy with her school and studies," Venkatachary proposed as Srinivasa was leaving for work that morning, to which Srinivasa happily agreed.

An excited Srinivasa made all the necessary travel arrangements for the trip, and the couple headed to Tirupati in a few days. As Kasthuri and Srinivasa sat beside each other on the train, they gazed dreamily into each other's eyes.

"Kasthuri, I still can't believe it's just you and me for the next few days," Srinivasa said as he gently squeezed Kasthuri's hand.

Kasthuri was equally excited and happy to go on this trip with her husband. Once the train reached Tirupati station, they took a bus to Tirumala Hill. The driver skillfully manoeuvred through the bends and turns on the way to the top of the hill. Kasthuri held her husband's hand and looked out the window with childlike excitement. The sight of spectacular waterfalls amid breathtakingly beautiful hills and various colourful birds flying around made the bus journey utterly enjoyable.

A cool breeze brushed against their faces as Kasthuri and Srinivasa alighted from the bus. Chants of *'Srinivasa, Govinda'* and *'Om Namo Venkateshaya'* echoed through the air, accompanied by the pleasant sounds of *Venkateswara Suprabhatam* and *Sri Vishnu Sahasranamam*. The couple felt they had been transported to a different world of calm and devotion. The divine fragrance of incense and camphor filled the air, along with the aroma of breakfast and filter coffee from the small hotels nearby.

They dropped their luggage at the cottage Srinivasa had booked, quickly bathed, and rushed toward the temple for Darshan. The tiredness from the long wait in the queue faded at the sight of the Lord, who looked divine, compassionate, and ready to embrace all who sought Him. The Lord's towering presence made tears flow down Kasthuri's cheeks. She felt a strange, strong connection to the Lord, who seemed to look at her with a reassuring, gentle smile, and a sense of devotion swept over her. The volunteers hastily ushered her out as she stood before the deity, gazing at Him wide-eyed and taking in His beautiful form.

The couple then headed to the Komala Vilasa hotel for lunch. Kasthuri had never eaten at a hotel before. She watched in wonder as the servers juggled multiple plates of food and numerous glasses of water while serving their customers. After spending another beautiful day in Tirupathi, they returned to Tadipatri feeling refreshed and rejuvenated.

A few days later, the school reopened for the start of the new academic year. Kasthuri quickly bathed and dressed in a simple sky-blue cotton saree with white stripes, ready for her first day at the new school. At 8:30 am sharp, Mallanna's horse cart promptly stopped by the gate to drop off Kasthuri and the other children at school.

The school here was a modest building, in contrast to the massive colonial-style structure of Hardwicke Mission. However, Kasthuri found the teachers here to be informal and affectionate compared to Hardwicke's highly formal and strict educators. Although language remained a barrier, Kasthuri managed to communicate with the two girls in her class, Ramya and Bhavani, using a mix of Telugu and English.

"How was school, Kasthuri?" asked a curious Srinivasa that evening. Kasthuri happily described her first day at school to Srinivasa, who listened with a smile.

"I must learn Telugu well to converse comfortably with my classmates and teachers at school. To do that, I need your help, *Ree.*"

Srinivasa smiled at his wife's determination to master the language. "Always at your service, my dear! What do you want me to do?"

"Henceforth, I want us to converse only in Telugu, and you need to correct me as needed."

"So be it!" Six months passed, and Kasthuri could now converse fluently in Telugu at home and school, too.

A few days later, on a particular morning, Kasthuri felt too tired to get out of bed. Srinivasa was surprised to find his wife still in bed, even after he had finished his yoga and bath.

"Kasthuri, are you feeling all right? It is so unlike you to be still sleeping after dawn!" Srinivas inquired as he sat beside his wife and touched her forehead to check for fever.

"I feel too weak even to sit up. I have been feeling nauseous for a few days. I feel giddy if I try to wake up."

Although Srinivasa was tough and courageous, seeing his dear wife unwell made him anxious. He informed his brother and sister-in-law of Kasthuri's condition and, on their advice, rushed to bring in the doctor, who gave them the good news of Kasthuri's pregnancy. Kasthuri was one month pregnant with her first child.

"Kasthuri, I have never been happier in my life! It almost seems unbelievable that a baby will soon be in our lives," an ecstatic Srinivasa said.

Kasthuri smiled but felt too unwell to truly experience the happiness herself. The good news was conveyed to Alamelamma through a letter, and her joy knew no bounds. Lakshmi ensured that Kasthuri rested well and pampered her endlessly. It had been almost two weeks since Kasthuri had been to school. Although feeling much better, Lakshmi insisted she rest for another week before returning to school.

With her family's love and support, Kasthuri completed her first trimester. She could now comfortably balance her schoolwork and home life. Her morning sickness had subsided, she could eat well, and she had started gaining a bit of healthy weight.

Months rolled by, and Kasthuri was four months pregnant. There was just a month until her annual examinations. Kasthuri planned her time well and studied hard. Srinivasa made it a point to accompany Kasthuri to the examination centre and bring her back home.

Seeing her husband patiently waiting for her at the examination centre gate every day filled Kasthuri with joy. On her final exam day, she walked happily toward him, and on the way home, they discussed the math paper together.

"Ree! You are a genius! The question paper had all those questions you had predicted would appear," Kasthuri said as she handed over the question paper to her husband.

"Did you check your answers thoroughly before submitting the answer sheet?"

"Yes, I did, and I'm sure to get all the answers right," Kasthuri replied confidently.

"I'm sure you will!" Srinivasa answered calmly. Kasthuri noticed that her husband wasn't his usual energetic and playful self. He seemed lost in thought.

"*Ree*! You seem unusually quiet today. What is the matter?"

"Kasthuri, Swamy *Garu* expects me to take care of something urgent that has come up in the company's Ceylon branch. I may have to leave for Ceylon in a week."

The sudden news took Kasthuri aback. It had been almost a year since the couple married. The wife and husband had become best friends, were practically inseparable, and led a blissful and happy life together.

"For how many days are you expected to be away?"

"3 months"

Tears rolled down Kasthuri's cheeks as she remained silent throughout the journey home, despite Srinivasa's attempts to reassure her. That night, too, Kasthuri lay on the bed without speaking to her husband.

"Kasthuri! My darling! Three months will pass in a blink. I promise to be back before the baby arrives. Do not worry," Srinivasa tried once more to reassure his wife.

"Now that my exams are over and I am free, I had hoped to spend much time with you. Also, I cannot imagine being away from you, especially when we expect our first child," she cried.

"I wouldn't want to be away from you either, Kasthuri! Swamy *Garu*, too, wouldn't send me away if it weren't an emergency," he said as he gently touched her shoulder. Kasthuri brushed his hand away and turned to the other side, sobbing.

The day of Srinivasa's travel arrived. He was to journey to Madras by train and then to Ceylon by boat mail, an express train and ferry service that connected Madras and Ceylon. It pained Srinivasa to see Kasthuri standing by the gate, looking dejected as he left. Kasthuri missed her husband tremendously, though everyone at home took great care of her.

In her husband's absence, life suddenly felt empty and dull. Kasthuri spent her summer vacation exploring new recipes and reading books from Venkatachary's fantastic collection.

That afternoon, when Venkatachary returned from school, he announced, "Kasthuri! Your matriculation results will be announced tomorrow!" The news excited everyone, especially Kasthuri.

The following day, as Venkatachary, Lakshmi, and Kasthuri sat on the verandah enjoying their morning coffee, a worker from Swamy Garu's office arrived with the good news that Srinivasa would be returning from Ceylone and arriving in Tadipatri the next day. The entire family rejoiced at the news. Kasthuri's happiness knew no bounds, and her heart danced joyfully. She thanked the Lord profusely for sending her husband home to be by her side when her matriculation results would be announced.

Kasthuri kept tossing and turning in bed that night. The thought of seeing her husband in a few hours thrilled her, and she woke before dawn. It took her a while to decide on the saree she would wear that day. Ultimately, Kasthuri chose a baby pink Benaras silk saree with silver zari flowers, as it was her husband's favourite among all her sarees.

"You look utmost beautiful in this saree, Kasthuri!" he would say as he looked at her without batting an eyelid.

Once she selected the saree, she quickly bathed, dressed with utmost interest, and walked into the kitchen. Lakshmi, who was in the kitchen preparing breakfast, looked at Kasthuri with a smile. "You look pretty, Kasthuri," she complimented.

Later, as Lakshmi helped cut the vegetables and grate the coconut, Kasthuri lovingly prepared her husband's favourite *Bisi Bele Bath*, the appetising aroma filling the entire house.

Kasthuri paced back and forth on the verandah, eagerly anticipating her husband's arrival. Venkatachary and Lakshmi observed Kasthuri's restlessness and excitement, and they exchanged meaningful smiles.

"Kasthuri, why don't you sit down for a while? We will know when the gate opens," Venkatachary quipped as he left for school.

As the wrought iron gate creaked, Kasthuri rushed out, followed by the equally excited children. As expected, a beaming Srinivasa walked toward them, and Kasthuri's heart skipped a beat at the sight of her beloved husband.

Srinivasa had longed to see his beloved wife, and there she was, standing in front of him, flashing a radiant smile, dressed in his favourite saree, looking extremely beautiful. They looked at each other with mixed emotions, as though they had much to say.

The tender moment was interrupted when the children surrounded their uncle with inquisitive questions about his trip and the goodies he had brought for them. As he distributed the gifts he had purchased, Venkatachary entered the house, looking pleased.

"Srinivasa, I'm happy you've chosen to return on this extremely special day."

"Special?" Srinivasa asked, looking puzzled.

Venkatachary said, "The matriculation results have just come in, and our Kasthuri has performed exceedingly well in the examination. She has topped the entire district of Anantapur." Venkatachary sounded overjoyed and proud of Kasthuri's achievement.

Kasthuri couldn't believe her ears. She knew she had performed well in all her exams, but never imagined she would be the district topper. Needless to say, she was overwhelmed with emotion. Srinivasa was elated and looked at his wife with immense pride.

After lunch, in the privacy of their room, Srinivasa pulled his wife into a passionate embrace. Kasthuri had longed for the warmth of her husband's intimate hold and felt loved and secure in his strong arms.

"Kasthuri, you have no idea how proud I am to be your husband. I would love to see you win more laurels and continue to make us proud." Her husband's happiness and encouragement brought tears to Kasthuri's eyes.

"You truly deserve a gift as beautiful as you! Don't you?" Srinivasa said, handing Kasthuri a beautiful jewellery box.

"Go on! " Open it, Kasthuri!" he said, his voice filled with excitement.

Inside the box lay an exquisitely crafted necklace and matching earrings embedded with green jade, pearls, and white stones. Srinivasa assisted Kasthuri in putting on the necklace and then led her to the mirror. He stood behind her, admiring her reflection.

"Beautiful!" he remarked. Kasthuri blushed, looked at her husband, and lovingly wrapped her arms around him.

"How have you been doing, my darling? How is our baby doing?" he inquired as he gently placed his palm on Kasthuri's stomach.

"He moves and kicks all night, and I can hardly sleep!" Kasthuri complained, and Srinivasa laughed heartily.

"Do you have any idea how much I've missed you?" Kasthuri asked, feigning anger.

"I do, Kasthuri! I have worked double shifts most days to be with you as soon as possible."

"Promise me that you will never leave me alone ever again!" Kasthuri demanded.

"I promise"!

Chapter 13

A month passed happily, and Kasthuri was now in the seventh month of her pregnancy. The family planned to conduct a grand *Seemantham* function for Kasthuri to celebrate her first pregnancy. The special day finally arrived, and so did all the relatives and friends. An ecstatic Alamelamma arrived with Rathna and Narayana, and Kasthuri was delighted to see them.

"Are you happy, *putta?*" was the first question Rathna asked her favourite niece.

"Yes, *Chikkamma,* very much!" Kasthuri sounded happy and content.

"The fact that you have done exceedingly well in your matriculation shows how supportive your family has been! I feel happy and reassured for you, *Putta!*" Rathna remarked happily, tears of joy welling up in her eyes.

"Rathna, isn't it hard to believe that our little girl is now all set to have a baby of her own?" Alamelamma asked her sister emotionally.

"Yes, *Akka*! But, no matter what, Kasthuri will always be our little girl!" Rathna gathered Kasthuri in a loving embrace and planted an affectionate kiss on her niece's cheek.

Srinivasa was determined to make this occasion special and memorable for his wife. He was well acquainted with the set decorators at Varaahi Studios. At his request, they adorned the entire living area with fresh flowers, mango leaves, silk fabric, and small, colourful lights. They even set up a small stage with a beautifully decorated chair for Kasthuri to sit on. Colourful cotton *jamkhanas* were spread out on the floor for the guests to sit.

Kasthuri looked as beautiful as a picture in a light purple *Kanjeevaram* saree adorned with stunning peacock motifs and a golden border. She wore the necklace and earring set Srinivasa had brought her from Ceylon. As Kasthuri slowly walked into the living area, holding Rathna's hand, everyone present couldn't take their eyes off the divinely lovely Kasthuri.

The women sang beautiful *Seemantham* songs while adorning Kasthuri's slender arms with multicoloured glass bangles and presenting her with baskets of fruits and sweets.

The guests were then led to the front yard, where a sumptuous dinner was served. Everyone enjoyed the incredibly delicious food and appreciated Srinivasa for the outstanding arrangements.

"Srinivasa, you have performed the *Seemantham* of your wife as grandly as one would perform a wedding," a distant cousin remarked appreciatively, while others agreed. All the guests left soon after, but not before showering Kasthuri with abundant blessings for a safe delivery.

After sending off the last guest, Srinivasa entered their room to find a tired Kasthuri deeply asleep on the bed. The moonlight from the window made her face shine, and she looked angelic. A profound love and affection for his wife swept over Srinivasa, and he gently kissed her forehead.

It was agreed that Kasthuri would travel with her family to Sakleshpur for the delivery. The topic for discussion now was how Kasthuri would manage her future studies.

"Srinivasa, since there is no college here in Tadipatri, students travel to Anantapur to study at the government college there," Venkatachary explained.

"But *Anna,* Kasthuri cannot travel to Anantapur by herself every day. Can she?"

"That's my concern, too. Fortunately, I happened to meet Rameshwaram *Master,* the headmaster of the government college in Anantapur, who is also a dear friend of mine. I spoke to him about Kasthuri, and he offered a solution." Venkatachary paused.

"He advised that under the given circumstances, Kasthuri could study at home with the help of tutors. He has graciously agreed to allow Kasthuri to appear for exams as a student of their college without attending regular classes. "

"Chalapathi *Sir* and other teachers from my school could guide Kasthuri with her preparation," he concluded. The idea seemed appealing to everyone, so a proper plan for Kasthuri's future education was outlined.

The next day, Srinivasa enrolled Kasthuri at the government college in Anantapur. The day after that was deemed auspicious for Kasthuri's journey to Sakleshpur. Bags and luggage were packed and ready for the trip. That night, Srinivasa seemed dejected and spoke little. The following morning, he continued to seem dull.

"*Ree*! I cannot bear to see you so sad! I hate to be away from you, too. Should I tell *Amma* that I won't go with her?"

"Don't be silly, Kasthuri! It is only right for you to be under your mother's loving care and guidance now."

"In that case, see me off with a smile! Will you?" she said, gathering her husband into a loving embrace. Srinivasa wrapped his arms lovingly around Kasthuri and pulled her closer. The couple had no intention of letting go of each other, but their moment of togetherness was interrupted by a knock on the door.

"Srinivasa, everyone's waiting. It's time to leave for the station," Venkatachary announced. As the train started to pull away from the platform, Srinivasa's eyes welled up as he watched Kasthuri wave to him until she could no longer see him.

Kasthuri's grandparents and Bhagwan were waiting at the gate to receive them. As soon as Kasthuri got down from the horse cart, an overjoyed Bhagwan ran toward his sister and excitedly rushed her in.

"Bhagwan, slow down! Kasthuri is no longer a little girl. She is carrying a child within her. You need to be careful!" his grandmother warned. Kasthuri, too, was thrilled to see her little brother.

As she walked up the stairs to the verandah, holding Bhagwan's hand, Kasthuri saw her father's armchair. It felt like her father had been waiting for her to come home. Kasthuri lovingly touched the chair and gently wiped away the little dust from it with the edge of her saree. "I'm home, *Appa!*" she muttered.

After a traditional *aarti*, she walked into the house where she was born and raised. Nostalgic and sweet memories associated with every nook of the house came rushing back to her, and it felt good to be home.

"Bhagwan, are you going to school every day and finishing your homework on time?" she asked her brother while savouring the hot breakfast their grandmother had served them all.

"Yes, *akka*! I haven't missed a single day since you left. I promised you, didn't I?" Bhagwan said with innocence and sincerity writ large on his face, to which Kasthuri beamed happily and lovingly touched his cheeks.

"*Akka*, Sir Albert was extremely pleased to hear about your matriculation results. He asked me to tell you he is immensely proud of you." The mention of Sir Albert made Kasthuri realise how much she missed her favourite teacher.

"Do you see Juliet at school?"

"Yes, *Akka,* every day. She was happy that you would come down to Sakleshpur and said she would come home to see you."

True to her word, Juliet came by to see Kasthuri a few days later, and it was an emotional reunion for the two friends. Like old times, they sat on the verandah chatting for hours until it was time for Juliet to leave.

Alamelamma and Kamalamma left no stone unturned in caring for the pregnant Kasthuri. They ensured Kasthuri had a balanced, nutritious diet and lovingly attended to all her cravings. One night, Kasthuri suddenly woke up with an intense craving for food.

"*Amma!*" She woke her mother, who was sleeping beside her.

"What is the matter, Kasthuri? Are you feeling unwell?" Alamelamma asked worriedly.

"I'm fine, *Amma,* but I wish to eat *Hesaru bele payasa,*" Kasthuri told her mother. Alamelamma smiled and promptly rushed into the kitchen, dishing out the delicious payasam for Kasthuri, who relished it to her heart's content.

Another day, she walked into the kitchen to see what her mother was preparing for lunch, only to find that the dishes made did not interest her.

"*Amma,* it's been a long time since I ate the *Vangi bath* you make. Could you please make that for me?" About half an hour later, Alamelamma placed a plate full of piping hot *vangi bath* in front of Kasthuri.

"*Amma,* as *Appa* always said, you truly have magic in your hands. This is the tastiest *Vangi bath* I have ever eaten," Kasthuri said, immensely enjoying her mother's pampering.

Rathna would bring Kasthuri's favourite butter biscuits and honey cakes from the Iyengar bakery near her school. Kamalamma made the choicest and most delicious *Ambodes* and potato *bajjis* whenever Kasthuri wished to eat them.

Once Bhagwan returned from school, he quickly finished his homework and spent the rest of his time with his sister, sharing stories about his friends and school. Occasionally, they enjoyed a quick game of *Chouka Bara*. In the evenings, the family gathered on the verandah, happily chatting while basking in the cool breeze. As Alamelamma crafted lovely garlands for the deities, Rathna and Kasthuri broke into a melodious *Krithi*. Days passed joyfully, and eventually, Kasthuri completed her full term, delivering a beautiful baby boy on a fine day.

Alamelamma lovingly held the baby close to her chest. "Kasthuri, the baby is a replica of your husband. He has the same nose and sharp features. I hope he grows up to be as bright as his father," she said.

"As bright as both his parents!" Rathna corrected her sister. "Here, Kasthuri, take a look at your beautiful boy!" said Rathna as she placed the baby beside his mother. A wave of immense love swept through Kasthuri as she saw the baby looking at her with half-open eyes and making soft, adorable sounds.

"Sweet boy, I am your mother!" she lovingly whispered to her baby, who seemed to respond with a blink of his tiny eyes. Bhagwan was too excited to leave the baby's side, even for a minute.

The news of the baby's arrival was promptly shared with Srinivas's family through a telegram. The overjoyed Srinivasa and Venkatachary set off for Sakleshpur immediately, arriving the following day. Lakshmi chose to stay with the children, though she longed to meet Kasthuri and the baby. Kasthuri couldn't wait to see her husband. As they entered her room, a smiling Srinivasa looked at Kasthuri with immense love and affection.

Venkatachary had by then taken the baby into his arms and looked at him fondly. "Srinivasa, here's your son. Go on, hold him!" he said, handing the baby to his brother. Srinivasa had carried his brother's children through their childhood, but this was his child, his flesh and blood. He felt a sense of happiness and pride as he held his son in his arms for the first time. "My son!" he said to himself, and a tiny tear of joy dropped from his eye as he kissed the baby. Kasthuri fondly watched her husband show affection to the little one.

"Kasthuri, I still cannot believe that God has blessed us with such a beautiful baby," Srinivasa said when they were alone.

"Everyone says he looks just like you. I feel so, too," Kasturi said with a smile.

Srinivasa beamed with joy and pride. "Hopefully, we will have a lovely daughter next time who will look just like you!" Srinivasa teased a blushing Kasthuri.

The brothers left for Tadipatri shortly after lunch, promising to return with Lakshmi and the children for the naming ceremony. The baby grew well under Alamelamma's expert care, and Kasthuri also gained some healthy weight.

"Amma, stop feeding me so much. Look, none of my old blouses fit me anymore," complained Kasthuri.

Three months later, in a beautiful ceremony attended by all their loved ones, the baby was named Krishna, much to everyone's delight. Kasthuri and the baby were set to return to her home in Tadipatri with her family the following day.

"*Akka*, I want to come with you too," Bhagwan said to Kasthuri."Please take me with you," he pleaded. Both Kasthuri and Srinivasa were more than happy to take Bhagwan along, and the duo convinced a reluctant Alamelamma to allow Bhagwan to accompany them. Srinivasa even assured her he would bring Bhagwan back to Sakleshpur whenever he wished to return.

Alamelamma had no choice but to give in, and needless to say, Bhagwan was thrilled and happily set off to Tadipatri with his sister and her family.

"Bhagwan, I expect you to be responsible and behave yourself in your sister's place. Do not trouble her, but instead, help her with little Krishna," Alamelamma strictly instructed Bhagwan at the railway station, to which Bhagwan nodded obediently.

Little Krishna was so used to being in his grandmother's warm cuddle that he cried his lungs out when Alamelamma handed him to Srinivasa as the train honked and prepared to depart. Alamelamma held back her tears as she watched her darling Kasthuri sitting by the window with baby Krishna in her lap, waving goodbye to them.

Chapter 14

The arrival of little Krishna brightened the house, and suddenly, everyone's life revolved around the baby. The children spent all their free time with him. The baby made cooing sounds and excitedly flapped his hands and legs when he saw his father. Srinivasa would pick him up and carry him to the front yard, where he showed him the cows in the shed and the birds that flew by. Lakshmi adored Krishna and lovingly cared for him during Kasthuri's study hours. Every other day, Venkatachary would happily bring home a new toy or rattle for his little nephew, even though Krishna was still too small to play with them.

Days passed happily, and baby Krishna reached his first milestone. He could now roll onto his stomach, look up, and smile, much to everyone's delight.

It had been nearly two weeks since Bhagwan was in Tadipatri. Due to his endearing nature, he quickly befriended the children, especially Jagannath. The two boys spent the entire day playing together.

While Bhagwan was enjoying himself in Tadipatri, Alamelamma began to miss her youngest child so much that she sent Narayana to fetch him from Tadipatri. Upon seeing his older brother, Bhagwan was reminded of home and his mother. He quickly bundled his clothes into a bag and was ready to go home. Kasthuri realised that he missed his mother and wanted to return to her.

"Bhagwan, when will you come back to see me?" Kasthuri asked her brother lovingly.

"As soon as school closes for summer vacations, *akka*," Bhagwan answered confidently as he prepared to leave.

The next few days after Bhagwan went, the house felt dull and deprived of his lively presence, and everyone missed him dearly.

Sunday was relatively free for Srinivasa, as he did not have to go to work. He was in the mood for a quick swim. "Kasthuri, I shall be back in a couple of hours," he said as he left. An expert swimmer, Srinivasa enjoyed swimming in the *Penna* River, just half a mile from home, whenever he had the time, usually on Sundays.

A few months passed, and little Krishna was now a 10-month-old baby, growing up happy, chubby, and adorable. Everyone in the house doted on him. He crawled quickly around the house and stood up with support. He recognised everyone, flashed the cutest smile, and raised his hands whenever he wanted to be picked up and taken out for a stroll.

Meanwhile, Kasthuri secured a distinction in her first year of FA, thanks to the invaluable guidance of Chalapathi Sir and her other tutors, as well as the immense support of her family. The admission formalities for her enrollment in the second year of college had also been completed. That afternoon,

Kasthuri sat on the verandah, feeding Krishna ragi porridge, when Srinivasa entered the house, looking angry and agitated. He sat down in the easy chair and closed his eyes.

"Kasthuri, could you get me a glass of water?" he asked. Kasthuri had never seen her husband, who was always calm and composed, in such a pensive mood. She walked in carrying little Krishna and returned with a glass of water, which she handed to Srinivasa, who continued to seem upset.

"What is the matter, *Ree?* You seem unhappy."

After a long pause, Srinivasa cleared his throat and answered, "Kasthuri, do you remember that Anna mentioned a few months back that a new teacher named Shantha had been recruited to the Zilla Parishad Primary School?" Kasthuri nodded in the affirmative.

"Swamy *Garu* has been spending much time at her house, neglecting his family and all business-related matters. He has spent all the money set aside for tax payments to buy her a palatial mansion in town."

"How irresponsible!"

"The tax department has been sending notices every day. Swamy Garu neither cares nor understands the seriousness of the situation, and I feel helpless."

"What do you plan to do now?"

"I plan to talk to him one last time tomorrow." The next day, Srinivasa left for the office very early in the morning to catch Swamy Garu before he stepped out. Luckily, Swamy Garu was at home.

"Swamy *Garu,* you need to understand the gravity of the situation. We have been receiving notices from the tax department every single day. They have warned of property attachment if the taxes are not paid." Krishna Swamy, whose mind seemed preoccupied, nodded absentmindedly.

"Swamy *garu*! Please understand that we will incur significant business losses if our properties are attached, and we may face bankruptcy. Do not let your family down. The words had the desired effect on Swamy Garu, and he looked at Srinivasa with an expression of alarm.

"What do we do now, Srinivasa?" he asked.

"Please sell the mansion you gifted to the teacher. The money we receive will help us pay the taxes we owe."

"Impossible!" Swamy roared. "Sell a couple of our properties at Anantapur and use that money to pay the taxes," he ordered. Srinivasa nodded reluctantly as anger and frustration swept over him. With incredible difficulty, Srinivasa managed to bail Swamy out of the crisis.

A couple of months passed, and Krishna was now a year old. He was walking and saying a few words. He would say '*Amma*' every time he saw Kasthuri, and she felt a profound motherly love for her son each time. Krishna would also say a few other words. Srinivasa would coax him to say *Nanna*. Still, the most Krishna managed to say was *Anna,* and Srinivasa would be disappointed.

"This boy manages to say all the words except *Naanna*," he would complain to his wife, like a little child, and Kasthuri would laugh heartily.

"He will! Very soon," she assured him.

The new academic year had begun, and Kasthuri's classes resumed with her tutors. Srinivasa also assisted her with her math work during the evenings. About a month had passed, and that evening, just as Srinivasa was winding up his work for the day, Krishna Swamy hurriedly approached him.

"Srinivasa, do you have the jewellery vault keys with you? Don't you?"

"Yes, as always, Swamy Garu!"

"Could you open the jewellery vault and bring me all of Soubhagya's (Swamy's wife's) jewellery?" Swamy asked in a pensive tone.

"*Ammagaru*," as Srinivasa would respectfully address Soubhagya, "has not mentioned any upcoming function or festival for which the jewellery would be needed," remarked a puzzled Srinivasa, who found this quite strange.

"Soubhagya doesn't need to know. Please bring me the jewellery immediately," Swamy said, creating a sense of urgency. Srinivasa immediately understood that Swamy wanted the jewellery for his newfound love interest. Not one to budge under pressure, Srinivasa refused.

"Swamy *garu,* when I joined you, you had clearly told me that the jewellery vault had to be operated only under the instructions of *Ammagaru* or your respected mother and no one else. Hence, I refuse to open it and hand over the jewellery to you," he said firmly. Srinivasa's bold refusal angered Swamy to no extent.

"How dare you refuse me, you snake? Is this what you give me in return for all the love I showered on you?" Swamy started to shout at the top of his voice, his entire body shaking in anger.

"I am and will always be grateful for your love and trust in me, and in return, all I can do is safeguard your assets and property from falling into the wrong hands."

"Do not think of yourself as a saviour of my family. You are just a bloody *Dewan;* your job is to follow instructions with your head bent and mouth shut."

Upon hearing the commotion, Swamy's wife, mother, and a few others rushed to the arguing duo. Srinivasa felt deeply hurt and shamed by Swamy's words. He turned to look at Swamy *Garu*'s mother, took the safety vault keys tied to his dhoti at the waist, and handed them to her.

"*Amma*, let me tell you that there is a great danger lurking, and if you do not take matters into your own hands, all your property and jewellery might fall into the wrong hands. Hence, I entrust the keys of the vault to you and leave with your kind permission." Srinivasa said as he swiftly walked out of Swamy garu's house and his life.

Kasthuri and the others at home were worried that Srinivasa, who usually returned from work by 5 pm, was still not home, even as the clock struck 7. Venkatachary was about to leave for Swamy *Garu*'s estate to find out what was causing the delay when Srinivasa walked in with a downcast face, looking sad and worn out.

"What is the matter, Srinivasa? Come, sit down." Venkatachary offered Srinivasa a chair as Kasthuri ran in to fetch a glass of water for him. Srinivasa drank the water, and as he handed the glass back to Kasthuri, he announced, "I have quit my job at Swamy Garu's estate." Needless to say, everyone was shocked. The mutual love and respect between Swamy and Srinivasa were common knowledge, so the news surprised them all. After a few minutes of silence, with a heavy heart, Srinivasa informed his family about what had transpired that evening.

"I shall not work at a place where I am not respected.", he declared firmly.

Just then, as if to make his dejected father happy, little Krishna took stumbling steps towards him, saying, *"Nanna,"* for the first time. An emotional Srinivasa picked up his son and showered him with kisses.

Chapter 15

With no compelling office work to keep him busy, Srinivasa decided to thoroughly delve into the affairs of the family-owned fields, mangroves, and coconut farms. He devoted most of his time and energy to enhancing the farms' yield and produce. Slowly but surely, Srinivasa became his cheerful old self.

As Kasthuri and Srinivasa sat down that afternoon to eat lunch, a worker from Swamy's estate arrived at the house, panting. It was evident he had come running.

"Ayya, Shantha teacher, has set herself ablaze and died at the hospital this morning. Swamy *Garu* is in a terrible state and wishes to see you immediately." The shocking news took aback both Srinivasa and Kasthuri.

"Where is Swamy *Garu* now?" Srinivasa asked.

"In his house at the estate."

"Kasthuri, let me visit Swamy Garu and see what the matter is," he said, hurriedly leaving with the worker. Swamy was sitting in the living room, holding his head. "Swamy garu!" Srinivasa called. Swamy looked up and hugged Srinivasa in a state of despair.

"Srinivasa, Shantha wanted all of Soubhagya's jewellery, and Amma refused to part with the vault keys. Hence, in retaliation, Shantha locked herself in and set herself ablaze. I was helpless," Swamy explained as he wept.

Srinivasa made Swamy sit down and tried to pacify him. "Swamy *Garu*, do not blame yourself for this unfortunate incident. It was not right of the teacher to take her own life for not getting something that never rightfully belonged to her."

"Srinivasa, you left your job here because of Shantha. Now that she is gone, please come back, as I feel lonely and helpless in your absence."

"Excuse me, Swamy *Garu*! I won't be able to join you back as your Dewan, but I shall always be there for you as a well-wisher. I kindly request that you take control of your emotions and return to living happily with your family." Srinivasa advised and walked out after offering Swamy Garu a few more words of comfort.

Back at home, with the commencement of the new academic year, Kasthuri's regular evening classes with her tutors had begun. Now that Krishna was a bit older, he played by himself happily with his toys. When the children were home, they played with him, and he entertained them with his sweet antics. Krishna would walk tiny steps to his mother or aunt when hungry or cranky, crying for their attention. In the evenings, after returning home from work, Venkatachary and Srinivasa wouldn't leave the toddler alone, even for a moment.

Two months passed, and Kasthuri's tutors were pleased with her progress in all subjects. However, Kasthuri had been feeling extremely unwell over the last few days, and a subsequent doctor checkup confirmed that Kasthuri was one month pregnant with her second child. While everyone at home rejoiced at the prospect of a little sibling for the naughty Krishna, Kasthuri appeared lost in thought even as she cradled Krishna to sleep that night in their room.

"Kasthuri, this time, I hope God blesses us with a little girl as pretty and bright as you," Srinivasa said dreamily. When he did not receive a response from Kasthuri, he looked up at her and found her lost in thought.

"Kasthuri, are you even listening to what I'm saying?" He asked as he gently shook his wife.

"*Ree*! According to the doctor, I'm one month pregnant, and it has been two months since the academic year began. Wouldn't the delivery date and the final examination date coincide, as they would happen in the same month?" Kasthuri's observation made Srinivasa think, too, and the fact shocked him.

"True, Kasthuri! I wonder why I didn't realise it earlier. What do we do?" Kasthuri nodded sideways and gestured as though to say she was confused, too. The following day, Srinivasa brought up the discussion with his brother.

"Well, it is a tricky situation, especially for an exceptional student like Kasthuri. But, at times, there is nothing much that one can do except surrender to His plan," Venkatachary advised.

Venkatachary further added, "Kasthuri, if you could look at the brighter side, you could continue your classes with your tutors and finish your portions now, when you are relatively free, so that you do not worry too much about balancing your classes and the baby next year."

Venkatachary's words sounded meaningful, making Kasthuri feel better. Soon, Kasthuri made peace with her situation and got on with her life, though the thought of losing an academic year would occasionally prick her. Nevertheless, she continued to study diligently for her second year of college and aimed to finish the entire syllabus before the baby arrived.

Months passed, and with her mother's loving care in the comfort of her paternal home in Sakleshpur, Kasthuri completed her full term and gave birth to a beautiful baby girl.

The baby girl inherited her mother's beautiful peaches-and-cream complexion, her father's sharp nose, and large, captivating eyes. Srinivasa named her Visalakshi, meaning the 'wide-eyed one'. Initially, Krishna felt insecure and cranky about the attention his baby sister received, especially from their parents. However, he eventually started to adore and care for her.

Little Visalakshi was growing up quickly and could now crawl all over the house while her brother playfully chased her. Although Lakshmi assisted Kasthuri with the two small tots, Kasthuri's hands were full as she cared for the babies and reviewed her lessons whenever she had time. Life continued happily for the couple with their two young children. Little Visala was nearly a year old, while Krishna was about to turn three.

As soon as he entered the house that evening, Srinivasa lovingly called out to his children, "Krishna! Visala!" as he always did. On hearing his father's voice, Krishna came running from the room inside, where he had been playing, shrieking excitedly, *"Naanna,"* while Visala crawled just as fast behind her brother. Srinivasa lovingly picked up his children and seated them on his lap. He soon became so lost in their world that he did not hear Kasthuri call him.

"Ree, I have been calling you for the last ten minutes. You are so full of your children these days that you seem to have forgotten me," Kasthuri complained.

"Even if the Sun were to rise in the West, Srinivasa could never forget Kasthuri. could he?" he quipped dramatically, to which Kasthuri rolled her eyes.

"If you could stop bluffing and take your bath, we could have dinner. It is ready to be served— Your Highness!" It was now Kasthuri's turn to be theatrical. The couple burst out laughing, and the children watching them appeared amused.

Kasthuri's final examinations for her second year of college were scheduled to begin the next day, and she was well prepared. However, she had to travel to Anantapur to take her exams. Kasthuri felt extremely anxious about leaving her two children for most of the day for six days.

"Kasthuri, it's only a matter of six days. Both Krishna and Visala are happy being around me. I assure you, I will take good care of them while you are away. So, relax and concentrate on your exams," Lakshmi assured a worried Kasthuri. Thanks to the immense support from her family, Kasthuri was able to write all her papers well. She felt happy and satisfied.

Srinivasa preferred to keep his Sundays free. Instead of the regular *Yogabhyasa,* he chose to go for a leisurely swim in the *Penna* River, half a mile from home. He would spend the rest of the day at home with his family. That Sunday, too, Srinivasa prepared to go to the *Penna.*

"Kasthuri! "I'm off to the river for a swim," he announced.

"*Ree,* I'm preparing all your favourite dishes for lunch today. Don't take too long; I'll be waiting for you."

"I will be back very soon, Kasthuri," Srinivasa promised before he left. Kasthuri had prepared a special Sunday lunch and sat on the verandah playing with the children, eagerly waiting for Srinivasa to return.

"Srinivasa is usually back much before lunchtime. It is already half past two. I wonder what is taking him so long today," Venkatachary pondered aloud as he sat in a chair, waiting for his brother.

"*Bavagaru,* I'm getting worried too. Let's ask Veera or Bhadra to run to the riverside and see what's wrong." Venkatachary nodded and called out to Veera.

"Veera, quickly go to the riverside where Srinivasa *ayya* usually goes for a swim and see what might be delaying him." Veera nodded and ran towards the gate.

On second thought, Venkatachary called out to him again. "Veera, wait! I shall come along too," he said, looking back at

Kasthuri and adding, "Child, I shall go and bring Srinivasa along myself; do not worry."

Though Venkatachary had assured Kasthuri, he began to feel a strange sense of anxiety as he walked briskly alongside Veera towards the river. Once they reached the riverbank, Srinivasa was nowhere to be seen, but they could see a crowd that had gathered in the distance.

"*Ayya*, shall we see why the crowd has gathered?" Veera asked. Venkatachary nodded, and as he started walking toward the crowd, he could feel his heart pounding in his chest. The group of men looked pensive as they discussed something. Veera recognised a couple of men who regularly swam with Srinivasa. Once they approached the crowd, they were both shocked and petrified at the sight of Srinivasa lying on the sand, lifeless, while a couple of fellow swimmers tried to revive him by pressing on his stomach and pounding on his chest.

"What happened to my brother? What are you doing to him?" Venkatachary demanded loudly.

"This morning, all of us, including Srinivasa ayya, started our swim together as always. We usually do not delve too deeply into the waters and return to the shore within an hour. Today, Srinivasa ayya excitedly ventured deeper into the river, and before we realised it, he was suddenly caught in a whirlpool. He was sucked into it even before any of us could help," a fellow swimmer explained how disaster struck, and the jaws of death forcibly grabbed Srinivasa into its fold.

"Only later, when he started to float, were we able to catch hold of him and bring him to the bank," the fellow swimmers added.

"It cannot be. My brother is an expert swimmer who has bravely faced such whirlpools and emerged unscathed," Venkatachary cried in disbelief.

"*Ayya,* sometimes, the river currents, especially towards the centre, are so strong that the best of the swimmers cannot fight them," one of the swimmers opined.

"No! Venkatachary roared! My brother cannot give up so easily." Venkatachary quickly leaned over his brother and checked for a pulse and a heartbeat. He could feel neither. "Srinivasa! Wake up!" he called out repeatedly as he shook his brother's lifeless body. With great difficulty, the men around convinced Venkatachary that Srinivasa had left this world.

"*Ayya,* your brother has passed away. His body is becoming cold and rigid. Please take him home," advised the fellow swimmers, who even organised a horse cart to carry Srinivasa's body back.

"Srinivasa!" Venkatachary cried aloud, "Your wife and children are eagerly waiting for you at home. How do I face them, and what do I tell them?" Venkatachary was inconsolable. Veera helped Venkatachary to his feet and, with assistance from others, carried Srinivasa's body to the cart.

"*Ayya,* let us take *Chinnayya* home," Veera said amidst tears.

In the meantime, Kasthuri had started to panic because neither her husband nor her brother-in-law had reached home yet. "Kasthuri, do not worry. They will be back home soon. Come sit," Lakshmi gently told Kasthuri, encouraging her to sit. Just then, she heard Bhadra wailing loudly at the gate. "*Ayya*," he cried.

Startled by his cries, Kasthuri sprang to her feet. She ran outside to see Veera and Bhadra, aided by a few others, carrying the lifeless body of Srinivasa through the gate toward the house. At the same time, Venkatachary followed behind with a forlorn expression.

"*Ree!*" shouted Kasthuri loudly as she ran towards her husband. A shocked Lakshmi followed her. Upon hearing the commotion, the children also ran out. Everyone was stunned beyond imagination as they looked at Srinivasa's body being carried in and placed on a mat in the verandah. Kasthuri ran alongside and collapsed next to the lifeless body of her beloved husband.

"*Ree,* wake up! *Bavagaru,* why is your brother not waking up? What happened to him?" she repeatedly asked, to which Venkatachary could only fall to the ground, weeping.

Forgive me, child! I failed to bring your husband back alive. The river's wrath has claimed your husband's life.

Kasthuri couldn't believe her ears and sat there, petrified by what she had just heard. She froze, her gaze fixed on her husband as if she were a statue. Despite the people around her weeping and wailing at Srinivasa's unexpected and untimely death, Kasthuri was too shocked to react. Just then, little Krishna, awakened from his nap, approached Kasthuri and sat on her lap, trying to wake his father.

"*Naanna! Naanna!*" he kept calling out to his father while gently shaking him, hoping his father would wake up and play with him. The scene melts Kasthuri, causing her to cry loudly.

"Kasthuri, Child, you need to pull yourself together and gain some strength for the sake of the children," Venkatachary said as he tried to console Kasthuri. At the same time, he struggled to come to terms with the sudden loss of his dear brother.

"My innocent children have been deprived of their father's love at such a young age. What wrong have they committed, *Bavagaru?*" cried Kasthuri. She recalled how happily her husband had left for his swim and was now lying lifelessly on the floor. The thought swept her with feelings of grief and helplessness.

Telegrams were sent to loved ones. Alamelamma, Rathna, and Kasthuri's siblings arrived just before the funeral. Everyone was in a state of shock and disbelief. Alamelamma's heart went out to her beloved daughter, who sat helplessly beside her husband's lifeless body.

"Kasthuri!" she called out, wailing as she ran to her daughter and gathered her in her arms. Her mother's voice and comforting touch resurfaced her emotions, causing Kasthuri to burst into tears. Rathna was distraught to see her favourite niece enduring such a great loss at such a young age.

It was now time for Srinivasa's final journey to the funeral ground. As his lifeless body was carried away, Kasthuri sprang to her feet and ran after him, crying.

"You had promised never to leave me alone. Why did you make that promise when you wouldn't keep it?" Kasthuri cried heartbreakingly. Alamelamma, Lakshmi, and all the other women there tried to console Kasthuri, but to no avail.

"Oh, Lord Venkata Ramana, why do you take away from me the ones I love the most? First, it was my father, and now it is my husband. What is it that you have against me?" Kasthuri continued to wail inconsolably.

In a short while, at the funeral ground, little Krishna was bathed and prepared to perform the last rites for his father. Venkatachary carried the innocent toddler in his arms and assisted him in lighting his father's funeral pyre. The scene moved everyone at the funeral and prompted them to reflect on the strange ways of God.

Chapter 16

Her aunt, siblings, and Manjula were great sources of strength and support for Kasthuri. However, after the thirteenth-day ritual, while her siblings returned to their respective homes, Alamelamma and Rathna decided to stay with Kasthuri for a few more days.

Kasthuri missed her husband terribly and remained dull and withdrawn. Their room, their cot, his clothes, his turban- everything reminded her of Srinivasa, and she would break down. At times, she saw a glimpse of her husband in her children. She would hold Krishna and Visala close to her chest and softly whisper to them, choked with emotion, "Little ones, you are all I have."

At times, her husband's memory would make her angry for leaving her alone, while at other times, it would overwhelm her with grief.

A month later, Narayana arrived from Mysore to accompany his mother and aunt back to Sakleshpur. That night, after dinner, as they all sat on the verandah, Alamelamma cleared her throat to speak.

"Anna!" she addressed Venkatachary, who looked at her questioningly. "Never in my dreams did I think that fate would

be so cruel to my darling daughter," Alamelamma said as she choked with emotion. Venkatachary nodded in agreement as he wiped a tear from his eye.

"I have the highest regard for you and Lakshmi for showering my daughter with great love and affection ever since she stepped into your house. Nevertheless, as a mother, I wish to have my daughter with me during this devastating phase of her life." Venkatachary and Lakshmi looked up at Alamelamma to understand what she was trying to convey.

"With your kind permission, I wish to take my daughter and her children back to live with us in Sakleshpur," she said.

"Alamelamma, Kasthuri is an integral part of this house and our lives, and little Krishna and Visala fill the void left by their father. However, I understand your concern for Kasthuri and do not wish to deny her your loving and reassuring care."

At this point, Kasthuri, who had been quietly listening to the conversation, said, "*Amma*, I had stepped into this house with my husband as a married woman. This is my house now. Though my husband is no longer alive, I wish to continue to live here with my children."

Alamelamma, Rathna, and Narayana tried their best to convince Kasthuri to return with them to Sakleshpur. However, Kasthuri was resolute in her decision, disappointing all of them, especially her mother, who began to sob.

"*Amma*, trust me. I will take good care of myself and the children. Please do not worry," she tried to reassure her mother. A helpless Alamelamma nodded, her eyes full of tears.

With heavy hearts, Alamelamma, Rathna, and Narayana departed for Sakleshpur the next day, leaving Kasthuri and her children behind in Tadipatri. Kasthuri suddenly felt lonely, but within a few days, she gathered her strength and resolved to be strong and courageous for the sake of her little ones.

Amid the grim situation at home, Kasthuri's second-year FA results were announced, and she passed with high distinction.

It had been two months since the tragic death of Srinivasa. The family was gradually coming to terms with his passing, except for little Krishna, who appeared to miss his father dearly and often fell ill. Venkatachary would remark sadly, "The child isn't able to express himself, but he seems to be thinking of his father."

Krishna had a fever for two days and slept in his mother's lap in the living area. Kasthuri gently patted him while Venkatachary walked into the living area.

"Kasthuri! The admission formalities for your B.Sc. need to be taken care of. With only the last few days left, we need to hurry up, child," Venkatachary announced. Kasthuri thought for a while as she looked down at her ailing firstborn in her lap. As though she had made up her mind, she looked up at her brother-in-law and said,

"*Bavagaru*! At this point, my children need me the most, and the only place I would want to be is around them." Venkatachary tried his best to convince Kasthuri to continue her education that year, but could not succeed.

"*Bavagaru*, by next year, the children will be a little older, and I shall continue my studies then," she said as she slowly got up and walked toward her room to put Krishna to sleep.

As days passed, Krishna gradually returned to his old, mischievous self. He ate well and played enthusiastically with his little sister. Since he was already three years old, Krishna was admitted to the primary section of the *Zilla Parishad* school on an auspicious day. With just a week remaining before school started, Kasthuri excitedly prepared new clothes, books, and footwear for Krishna.

Krishna went to school every day, happily and without throwing a tantrum. He would return to his mother and share endless stories about the day's events at school. Kasthuri remembered her days at Hardwicke and how she enjoyed sharing her school stories with her father. The memory of her father brought tears to her eyes.

Meanwhile, on the home front, Venkatachary found it very difficult to manage the fields, farms, and other family-owned properties that Srinivasa had managed efficiently and smartly up to that point. While Srinivasa had a knack for handling the workers and extracting work from them, the farm workers took advantage of the soft-spoken Venkatachary.

The farms and fields stood neglected, even though Venkatachary paid them their wages regularly. While Srinivasa managed the finances with an iron hand, knowing precisely how much to spend and what to expect, Venkatachary was a novice in these matters. When the workers demanded money, citing expenses such as pipeline repairs and purchasing fertilisers and seeds, an unsuspecting Venkatachary parted with the sum.

"Ramalinga, how much have we received from mango sales this summer? You haven't handed over the amount to me yet," Venkatachary asked the supervisor at the mangrove.

"*Ayya*, we have not had any proper yield this year due to infestation. Hence, no harvest could be sold," he lied without a hint of guilt.

A similar story unfolded at other farms and fields. Vast amounts of money had been spent, yet not a single penny was received. Venkatachary was now a worried man.

"Lakshmi, we are heading to a financial crisis. Apart from my meagre salary, we have not received a single penny from our properties," he explained to a shocked Lakshmi.

"The household expenses, children's fees, and their clothes need to be taken care of, and I don't have enough money for any of these," Venkatachary sounded helpless. Needless to say, Lakshmi was now worried too.

"What do we do now? Should we discuss the matter with Kasthuri?" a worried Lakshmi asked.

"We cannot keep Kasthuri in the dark about the situation."

That night, after the children had gone to bed, Venkatachary and Lakshmi sat down with Kasthuri. They explained the situation and the family's financial woes to her. Kasthuri felt both shocked and disturbed. It was yet another major blow that fate had dealt her after her husband's death.

Venkatachary's monthly salary had become the sole source of income. Kasthuri and Lakshmi managed the household on a tight budget. Veera, Bhadra, and other household staff members were instructed to seek employment elsewhere. Mallanna's horse cart was halted, requiring all the children, including Little Krishna, to walk to and from school each day. Tutors were let go. Purchasing new clothes for festivals and birthdays was discontinued. Instead of preparing two curries, only one was cooked at home.

"*Amma*, my footwear broke on the way from school, and I had to walk barefoot in the hot Sun. Look, I have blisters on my soles," Krishna cried in pain one day.

Kasthuri made Krishna lie down in her lap, and as she applied soothing butter on the blisters, her eyes welled up. "Krishna, *Amma* shall buy you a pair of new, shiny slippers in a few days," she assured her crying son, though she knew that it was the fag end of the month and a new pair of footwear could not be afforded at that point.

"Why in a few days, *Amma*? Why not today?" demanded a weeping Krishna.

"*Kanna*, the shopkeeper doesn't have slippers that fit you right now. He will be getting them in a few days. Do not worry; until then, *Amma* will carry you home from school every day," she assured him, and the tired child soon fell asleep.

"The situation at home is getting from bad to worse. What do we do now, *Bavagaru*?" Kasthuri asked Venkatachary that night during dinner.

"The only way out is to sell our properties," Venkatachary said helplessly.

Meanwhile, amid the gloomy state of affairs, a ray of hope emerged in the form of Venkatachary's new job offer as headmaster of the Government City High School in Hyderabad, which included a pay increase of 50 rupees. That evening, Venkatachary discussed this happy development with Lakshmi and Kasthuri.

"When are you expected to report for the new job?" asked Lakshmi.

"By next week. Once the financial matters here in Tadipatri are settled, all of you can shift with me to Hyderabad," Venkatachary assured. Subsequently, all properties, except for the house, were sold within four months, but at prices lower than market value.

"*Bavagaru*, it would be wise to use a portion of the money to purchase a house in Hyderabad before it gets spent on household expenditure. We could avoid spending on house rent every month," Kasthuri advised.

With help from a few friends, Venkatachary purchased a reasonably spacious house in Hyderabad, and it was now time for the entire family to relocate to Hyderabad.

Kasthuri entered her room and sat on her cot, holding her husband's turban, coat, and clothes in her lap. "*Ree*, I trust you to watch over me and the children wherever we are. You will! Won't you?" she muttered emotionally as she lovingly touched her husband's belongings, which she had carefully packed in her luggage to take to their new house in Hyderabad.

Chapter 17

It was September 1929. Venkatachary, Lakshmi, Kasthuri, and the children boarded the bus to Hyderabad from Anantapur. After a long, tedious journey, the bus had just entered Hyderabad when it screeched to a sudden halt. As the passengers looked out the windows to understand why the bus had stopped, they saw a group of men protesting on the road amidst slogans of *'Vande Mataram'* and *'Bharat Mata Ki Jai,'* being beaten mercilessly and dragged away by the Nizam's troops.

"Unfortunately, the freedom fighters in Hyderabad need to fight not only the British but also the tyrannical *Nizam*." Venkatachary thought to himself sadly.

The house in Hyderabad was spacious enough to accommodate all of them comfortably; however, it was not as vast and palatial as their house in Tadipatri. Venkatachary's colleague at the school, Subbaiah, and his wife, Sharada, lived only a few houses away. Subbaiah and Sharada were immensely helpful to the family as they settled into their new surroundings. Subbaiah and Venkatachary became good friends and often went on morning walks together.

While Krishna and Jagannath were admitted to the City Government School, Aruna and Padmini awaited their admission to the first-year FA.

"Kasthuri, child! Now that we are all more or less settled, why not consider continuing your education?"

"I was thinking about it too, *Bavagaru!*" Kasthuri answered. She also longed to return to her studies and pursue her graduation in mathematics.

"Very well then! I shall take you and the girls to college to finish the formalities and pay the fees in a week," Venkatachary said, much to Kasthuri's happiness.

As she walked into her room, Kasthuri excitedly picked up Krishna, who was playing with a wooden toy car, and began dancing with him. "Krishna, *Amma* is going to be a graduate soon!" Kasthuri shared her happiness with her little son. Although amused, Krishna did not quite understand the reason for his mother's excitement; nevertheless, he revelled in it too and danced along.

Sadly, fate had its plan. Venkatachary's oldest child and the couple's favourite daughter, Annapurna, stayed in Delhi with her husband, a military doctor, and their young daughter, Shashi. That afternoon, Venkatachary received a telegram that devastated the family. Annapurna's husband suffered grievous injuries and died after being thrown from the horse he was riding.

Venkatachary rushed to Delhi immediately. Annapurna's in-laws had come down from Kakinada to attend their son's funeral. They left without even saying goodbye to their daughter-in-law or little Shashi. It seemed they had washed their hands of responsibility and wanted nothing to do with their older son's family. Their insensitive behaviour greatly hurt Venkatachary and Annapurna. He consoled his distraught daughter and travelled back to Hyderabad with Annapurna and Shashi in tow.

Two additional members meant an extra financial burden for a family struggling to manage expenses. A few days after Annapurna and her daughter had settled in well, Kasthuri spoke to Venkatachary.

"*Bavagaru,* you mentioned the other day that your school has a vacant Math teacher position. Would it be possible for me to get the job since I have already passed my FA with distinction?"

"Kasthuri! I understand you want to take on this job to help us avoid an inevitable financial crisis. While I appreciate your concern, it would make me very guilty if you gave up your dream of graduating for the sake of this family." Venkatachary sounded extremely sad.

"*Bavagaru,* after my husband's death, I chose to stay with all of you because I consider you all my family. Similarly, I would be happy if you consider me a part of your family and allow me to share all responsibilities."

What about your dream of graduating, Kasthuri? It makes me feel helpless to witness your dream being crushed repeatedly.

"*Bavagaru*, we are all mere players in the hands of fate. If I were to graduate, I would surely do so someday. Please do not feel guilty for something that is beyond your control."

Venkatachary was amazed by Kasthuri's maturity, sense of responsibility, and decision-making at such a young age.

Within the next week, Kasthuri received her appointment letter as a secondary school Mathematics teacher at the City Government School. Kasthuri held the letter in her hands and read its contents happily over and over again. She was to draw a salary of thirty-five rupees a month and it made her feel empowered.

"I would hand over three-fourths of her salary to Lakshmi Akka and save one-fourth for a rainy day," she decided and conveyed the same to Lakshmi.

A new leaf had turned in Kasthuri's life, and the prospect of teaching Mathematics, her favourite subject, to young children excited her. The city government school in Hyderabad was a beautiful building designed in the European style, featuring Islamic-style arches and domes. Kasthuri's colleagues were primarily male, with only one other woman on the staff.

Ramani, the teacher who taught Telugu, was almost the same age as Kasthuri, and they soon formed a strong bond. They would sit in the staff room, spend their lunch hour eating together, and chat about their families.

Kasthuri enjoyed teaching the children, and the children loved Kasthuri's classes. When the last bell rang at three, she quickly said goodbye to Ramani and walked home with Krishna and Jagannath in tow.

"Vishu!" she called out as she walked in, and little Visala dashed into her mother's arms. A little while later, after she had freshened up, Kasthuri sat in the living room playing with Visala, while Lakshmi lovingly handed her a hot cup of coffee and a small plate of snacks.

"*Ahaa! Mirapakaya bajji*! When did you manage to make these, Akka? They are delicious!" Kasthuri appreciated the snacks as she relished them.

"Annapurna has made these Kasthuri!"

"Oh really! I never knew our Annapurna could cook so well!"

"Neither did I! As you know, she has always been the pampered child. We never allowed her to do any chores at home. She seems to have learned to cook after her wedding," Lakshmi said, while Kasthuri nodded.

Annapurna enjoyed cooking so much that she gradually took over the cooking duties at home and treated her family to wholesome and delicious food.

Due to a tight financial situation at home, Aruna and Padmini were unable to join FA, just as Kasthuri had been unable to join the first year of graduation. Lakshmi was eager to get the girls married, so the couple searched for suitable alliances. Soon, their marriages were arranged with well-qualified boys.

With no funds to hold the two marriages, the beautiful ancestral house in Tadipatri had to be sold, and a portion of the proceeds was used to conduct the weddings.

"*Bavagaru,* why don't we invest the remaining money in buying a small house nearby and renting it out? The rental income could be used towards the children's education," Kasthuri suggested. A small two-room house was soon purchased near their home. Thankfully, the rent received from the tenants added to the family's monthly income.

Years rolled by. Krishna was now 12 and in the final year of middle school, while Visala was 10 and in the second year of middle school. Both children were exceptionally bright and hardworking. Krishna took a keen interest in mathematics, while Visalakshi's favourite subject was science. Kasthuri was promoted to high school as a mathematics teacher with a pay increase of 30 rupees.

Kasthuri and the children spent their summer vacations in Mysore every alternate year. Alamelamma had not been well for the past few years and had since been living with Narayana and Manjula in Mysore. Bhagwan joined the Army against the family's wishes and was now stationed in faraway Shimla. Rathna's parents had passed away due to age-related ailments, and she lived alone in Sakleshpur. Whenever Kasthuri visited Mysore, Rathna would also come over and spend a few days with her and the children.

"*Chikkamma,* why don't you shift with me to Hyderabad?" Kasthuri would plead.

"I will eventually come to stay with you, my dear, but not right away," the highly independent and self-reliant Rathna would respond firmly.

Back in Hyderabad, although Kasthuri was happy and content with her job, the desire to complete her graduation still burned brightly within her. She had been saving a bit of money each month to fund her graduation, which she planned to pursue as a private student while continuing to work at the school. She opened the black leather bag where she had been saving the money and began counting the notes; her face lit up.

"This is enough to fund the fees for all three years of graduation. I shall inform *Bavagaru* this Sunday and enrol myself in the course," she thought happily. "Graduate Kasthuri," she muttered to herself dreamily, and the sound of it made her happier.

Chapter 18

The Sun's early rays fell on Kasthuri's face, and she woke up hurriedly, a little later than usual. She quickly bathed, completed her kitchen chores, and rushed to wake the children. "Krishna! Visala! Wake up, my darlings!" she called out, pulling out a fresh set of school uniforms for the children. Visala woke up lazily, while Krishna remained asleep. This seemed unusual since Krishna would usually wake up at the first call before Visala did.

"Krishna! What is the matter, *Kanna?* Why don't you wake up?" Kasthuri asked as she gently shook him, and she was taken aback. Krishna was burning with a high fever and opened his eyes with great difficulty.

"Amma, my stomach is hurting, and I feel too weak to wake up," he said.

"Vishu, run out and call *Peddayya,*" Kasthuri instructed her daughter as she began to panic. Upon seeing Krishna's condition, Venkatachary immediately rushed out to bring the RMP doctor, Thirupathaiah, who arrived and checked on Krishna.

"The boy is down with Typhoid. We need to start his treatment without any delay. I shall provide him with all the necessary medicines, and at home, he should be given a bland diet until the fever subsides. Strictly no spice and oil," he instructed.

"How long might it take for the fever to subside, Doctor?" Venkatachary enquired worriedly.

"About a week."

"*Amma,* could you stay with me?" Krishna begged his mother as he held her hand tightly.

"Krishna, I'm not leaving your side until you're well. Do not worry. I have also applied for a week's leave." Kasthuri patted her son's hand reassuringly.

Kasthuri did not allow Venkatachary to pay for the medicines or the doctors' fees. She insisted she would pay for Krishna's treatment from her savings.

Krishna's fever subsided in about a week but was still extremely weak. After two more weeks of rest and medication, a healthy Krishna resumed attending school.

That evening, Krishna returned home joyfully and told his mother about a school trip to the Burra Caves near Visakhapatnam that had been organised.

"*Amma,* all my friends are going on this trip, " he said. Although the school had arranged trips in previous years, Krishna could never join his friends due to the tight financial situation at home. However, this time, he hoped to go.

"Do you want to go too, *Kanna?*" Kasthuri asked, sensing Krishna's interest and enthusiasm.

"Yes, *Amma*, but I do not want the trip expenses to disturb the household budget." Krishna was mature enough to understand the family's financial difficulties.

"I shall pay for the trip from my savings. It wouldn't affect the household budget. Do not worry." Kasthuri assured her son, much to his delight and excitement. The fees for the trip were paid, and a happy Krishna embarked on his first trip with his friends.

Kasthuri, however, realised that more than a quarter of her savings had been spent on Krishna's treatment and the school trip. Unfortunately, the unexpected expenses meant that her plan to resume her studies would take a backseat yet again.

"My children's health and well-being are of utmost importance. My dreams can wait," she convinced herself, shoving the remaining money back into the purse.

Meanwhile, it was celebration time at the Venkatachary household after years of hardship and challenges. Jagannath's wedding was unexpectedly arranged with a lovely girl named Sarala, and the wedding took place shortly thereafter, bringing great joy and happiness to the entire family. The newlywed couple soon relocated to Nizamabad, where Jagannath worked as an accountant at the Nizam Sugar Factory.

Another year passed, and Krishna was now 13 years old and in the 4th form. He was the favourite student of all his teachers and consistently placed first in every subject each year. Krishna reminded Kasthuri of her younger self and her days at Hardwicke Mission.

Visala, too, was a good student; however, her mother constantly reminded her to complete her homework and study regularly for her tests. Her daughter reminded Kasthuri of her mischievous brother, Bhagwan.

Kasthuri eagerly awaited the announcement of enrollment and fee payment dates for private students in the first-year degree course, and they were finally announced. Twenty days were available to complete the admission formalities. Five days had passed, as Kasthuri was busy with the children's annual examinations at school. She was determined to complete the admission formalities in the next few days.

"Telegram!" yelled the telegraph boy standing at the gate. Venkatachary went out anxiously to sign for and receive the telegram, wondering who might have sent it. Narayana from Mysore was the sender, and the content read, "Mother serious. Start immediately." By then, Kasthuri and Lakshmi had also come up to the gate. Venkatachary quietly handed the telegram to Kasthuri. An anxious Kasthuri rushed to Mysore along with her children on the next available train.

Alamelamma was on her deathbed when Kasthuri and the children arrived. It was as though she was holding on to dear life, driven by her wish to see her youngest daughter. All her other children were around her. Kasthuri ran to her mother, sobbing, and Alamelamma gently caressed her youngest daughter's face and kissed her hand affectionately. She signalled for the children to come closer and touched their heads as if to bless them.

"*Amma*, now that Kasthuri is here, you must get well soon and spend a lovely time with your favourite daughter."

Narayana tried to sound motivational but choked with emotion as he spoke. Alamelamma looked one last time at Kasthuri and then left the world.

Kasthuri and her siblings were devastated by the loss of their dear mother. Rathna, who was extremely close to her older sister, was inconsolable as well. The siblings and their aunt became each other's sources of strength and weakness. Kasthuri and her children remained until the 13th-day ritual and prepared to return to Hyderabad the following day.

Upon reaching Hyderabad, Kasthuri felt dull and depressed for the next few days. With her mother gone, she felt orphaned. However, her work at school and being around her children helped her heal slowly. As Kasthuri searched for a matching blouse in her wardrobe that day, her eyes landed on the black leather bag. She was immediately reminded of the enrollment dates for the degree course, and a wave of panic swept over her.

"Oh no! It is almost a week past the last date," she suddenly realised. "I have missed the chance this time, too," she thought, dropping onto the cot helplessly as tears rolled down her cheeks. She did not realise how long she sat there weeping until the loud laughter of the children playing around the house brought her back into this world.

"It is probably not my destiny to graduate. Why else would God create a grave situation each time just when it is time for enrollment?" she thought. "He probably wants me to live my dream through my two children. So be it! I bury my graduation dream here and now, forever," she said to herself firmly.

Days turned into weeks, weeks became months, and months became years. Krishna was now a handsome twenty-year-old man. He was the spitting image of his father and had sharp features reminiscent of Srinivasa. "Junior Srinivasa," Venkatachary would fondly call him. However, he did not inherit his father's dark complexion; instead, he was fair like his mother. Krishna was in his final year of a bachelor's degree in mathematics and was on the verge of graduating.

Visala was now 18 and had grown into a beautiful young lady. She inherited the best features from both her parents and looked lovely. She had her father's large, beautiful eyes, her mother's endearing smile, a peaches-and-cream complexion, and long, thick, lustrous hair.

Visala had applied to Osmania Medical College to pursue a degree in medicine and was awaiting the results. Every morning, Venkatachary walked to the college with his friend Subbaiah to check whether the list of selected candidates had been posted.

"Kasthuri! Visala!" he called out excitedly as he rushed home from his walk that morning. Kasthuri and Visala hurried to the living room to see what the matter was, along with Lakshmi and Annapurna from the kitchen.

"*Peddayya,* what happened?" Visala asked curiously.

"Open your mouth, child!" he said as he stuffed a piece of the laddu into Visalakshi's mouth.

"Lakshmi! Kasthuri! Our Visala has secured a merit seat for studying MBBS at Osmania Medical College. She will be the first doctor in our family," Venkatachary happily announced.

Visala shrieked in excitement and gave her mother a tight hug. Kasthuri's eyes welled up with happy tears, and she kissed Visalakshi's forehead lovingly. "Your hard work has paid off, "Vishu! I feel so proud of your achievement," she said.

"Your hard work has paid off, too, Kasthuri. Years of hard work and dedication!" Lakshmi said as she pulled Kasthuri closer in a loving embrace. Venkatachary nodded as though in agreement with what his wife said.

"*Bavagaru*, how much fees should we pay each year?" Kasthuri enquired.

"Nothing at all, Kasthuri. Our Visala secured a free seat owing to her exceptional marks in FA. The only expenses would be buying books, which could be purchased secondhand. So, we are not incurring any exorbitant expenses."

Kasthuri felt relieved and happy that her daughter could pursue her professional education without financial difficulties.

Visala was so excited by the prospect of becoming a doctor that she joyfully danced around with her cousin, Shashi.

"Vishu, just wait until you have to dissect frogs and snakes. Let's see if you can still dance after that," Krishna playfully teased his sister, prompting hearty laughter from everyone.

Chapter 19

The final-year B.Sc. results were to be announced the following day, and Krishna was so anxious that he couldn't sleep, nor did he let his mother and sister sleep that night. "*Amma,* do you think I'll fare well in the results tomorrow?" he woke Kasthuri and asked.

"*Kanna,* you have studied hard and performed well on your exams. Why, then, wouldn't you fare well?" Kasthuri assured him and slowly went back to sleep.

Krishna woke his sister after a few hours of tossing and turning in bed. "Vishu, wake up!" he called softly, gently shaking her out of sleep. "What is it, Anna?" Visala asked as she sat up on her bed.

"Vishu! I feel anxious about the results coming out tomorrow. Do you think I shall pass with a first division?"

"Of course, *Anna.* You will do exceptionally well. Do not worry," Visala assured before going back to sleep.

Visala's words filled Krishna with confidence, but only briefly. He woke her again to ask the same question. Visala reassured her brother, though she sounded slightly irritated about being disturbed. When Krishna woke her for the third time, she was furious. *"Amma!"* she called out to her mother. Kasthuri woke up and was surprised to see her children awake at such a late hour.

"What is the matter, Visala? Why aren't you both asleep?"

"Why don't you ask your dear son that question? He seems overtly excited about tomorrow's results. Neither does he sleep nor let me sleep," complained Visala. "I intend to catch at least a few hours of sleep. I am going to sleep in Shashi's room," she declared, gathering her pillow and blanket before walking out in a huff after giving her brother a death glare.

Kasthuri looked at Krishna, sitting on his bed with an innocent expression, wondering why his sister had overreacted, and she laughed out loud.

Kasthuri encouraged, "*Kanna*, believe in yourself and have faith in God; all will be well." Krishna nodded.

"Now, why don't you catch some sleep and let me sleep too?"

Venkatachary accompanied Krishna to the Government Degree College the following day to check the results. A couple of hours later, the duo returned, their faces brimming with happiness and hands holding boxes of sweets.

"Kasthuri! Your son has passed his BSc with a high distinction," Venkatachary proudly announced.

The news overwhelmed Kasthuri, causing her to collapse into a nearby chair, tears streaming down her cheeks. Krishna rested his head on his mother's lap while Kasthuri tenderly stroked his hair. "Only if your father were to be alive today, he would be immensely proud of you, *Kanna,* just as much as we all are," Kasthuri said, her voice choked with emotion.

"What next, Krishna?" Venkatachary asked his nephew about his future plans during dinner that evening.

"I wish to pursue my post-graduation in mathematics, *peddayya,*" Krishna answered. He secured a seat at Osmania University in Hyderabad for his post-graduate studies in Mathematics.

Although Krishna enjoyed his time at the University, classes were held irregularly and were frequently suspended due to political tensions and uprisings in the state.

The Indian freedom struggle reached its climax in 1947. After decades of resistance against British rule, India finally attained independence on August 15, 1947.

"Why isn't anyone celebrating the happy occasion of the country's independence, *Peddayya*? The roads seem deserted, as though there is a curfew," Krishna wondered.

"The *Nizam* has banned all public celebrations, Krishna! His troops are arresting anyone who dares to come out to celebrate the country's independence. I hope the Nizam sees some sense soon and accedes Hyderabad to the Indian Union," Venkatachary expressed his wish.

However, the ban on public celebrations did not deter people from joyfully celebrating the country's independence within the confines of their own homes. Subbaiah invited

Venkatachary and his family, along with a few of his other friends and their families, for a grand celebration at his house, where they rejoiced in the country's independence together over a sumptuous lunch and cheerful conversations.

Many months passed amidst peasant uprisings and people demanding that the *Nizam* join India. That morning, Venkatachary hurried home from his walk, wiping the sweat from his forehead. He took the glass of water Lakshmi handed him and gulped it down hastily. Kasthuri, walking by, noticed the tension on Venkatachary's face. "What is the matter, *Bavagaru?*" she inquired.

"Kasthuri! Lakshmi! Do not step out for a few days, nor let the children out. It seems the *Razakars* are creating havoc and mercilessly slaughtering all those who dare to cross their path, not even sparing the women and innocent children. We must lock ourselves in and keep chilli powder and knives handy for self-defence." Venkatachary cautioned his family. Like all their neighbours, the family mostly stayed indoors for the next few weeks as fear and insecurity gripped them.

A couple more weeks passed, and on 17 September 1948, a loud knock on their door that evening startled everyone. Alarmed, Venkatachary hurried the women in the house into one of the rooms and instructed them to lock the door behind them.

"Do not open the door until either Krishna or I ask you to," Venkatachary cautioned them as they rushed in.

There was another loud knock on the door while Krishna and he waited anxiously in the living room. To their relief, they heard Venkatachary's friend, Subbaiah, calling out, "Venkatachary, open the door." As Venkatachary opened the door, Subbaiah happily hugged him.

"Did you hear the news?" he asked excitedly. The *Nizam* has surrendered to the Indian government. Hyderabad is now officially a part of the Indian Union." Subbaiah happily shared the good news with Venkatachary, handed him a box of laddus, and left to share the news with his other friends.

"Krishna, come, let's get sweets and distribute them in the neighbourhood," an ecstatic Venkatachary urged Krishna. The day was nothing short of a festival at the Venkatachary household. The family and all the people of Hyderabad celebrated their liberation in a true sense.

The subsequent academic year went smoothly without disturbances, and Krishna passed his exams with flying colours. He was now a postgraduate in Mathematics, the family's first postgraduate.

The next day was *Ugadi*, the Telugu New Year, and Krishna's outstanding post-graduation results made the festival even more special. The Venkatachary household was filled with festive cheer. Jagannath and his wife, Sarala, had come home from Nizamabad to celebrate the festival with their family, which added to everyone's happiness. Lakshmi completed her puja and entered the living room with a large bowl of *Ugadi Pachadi*, a bitter-sweet-sour concoction made during Ugadi, with each taste representing a facet of life.

Visala and Shashi attempted to sneak out the main door onto the terrace to avoid tasting the awful *Pachadi*. Krishna pulled them back and made them stand before Lakshmi.

"*Peddamma,* these two girls were trying to escape to the terrace to avoid eating the *Pachadi* you made. Please feed the *Pachadi* to these two first as a punishment," Krishna suggested to his aunt, who played along with his nephew's tunes and forcibly fed the bittersweet *pachadi* to the two girls.

After gulping it down with great difficulty, the two annoyed girls caught hold of Krishna. They ensured that Lakshmi fed him not one but two spoons of the ghastly concoction. As Krishna struggled to eat it, the girls laughed triumphantly.

As the family enjoyed the festive lunch, Jagannath mentioned that the Reserve Bank of India's Hyderabad branch was recruiting eligible graduates and postgraduates for the officer post. "It is an excellent opportunity, Krishna. Why don't we approach them with your mark sheets and certificates?" Jagannath suggested, and Krishna immediately agreed.

As planned, Jagannath accompanied Krishna to the bank the next day. They were directed to the recruitment cell, which reviewed Krishna's certificates and scheduled an interview for the following day. Although Krishna was a bit nervous, he answered all the questions during the interview with great confidence. Within a week, Krishna received an appointment letter requesting him to report for his duties as a Junior Officer immediately, much to his family's happiness.

"Your mother's life has been nothing short of a penance. I hope you care for her with love and respect for the rest of her life. "

"I shall take good care of not only *Amma* but also all of you, *peddayya,*" Krishna answered emotionally.

Visala had entered the fifth and final year of her medical course, while Krishna was happily working at the bank. Annapurna's daughter, Shashi, had also graduated and secured a job at the Central Government's Income Tax department. Shortly after, she married a distant relative who worked as an engineer in a private firm, much to Annapurna's happiness.

Kasthuri was now promoted to the post of assistant headmistress at the Government High School and received a monthly salary of eighty rupees.

One fine morning, a middle-aged couple unexpectedly visited Venkatachary's home. "*Namaskaram*! I am Sadasiva Sarma, and this is my wife, Kamakshi," the man introduced himself and his wife. Venkatachary welcomed them inside and offered them glasses of water after they were comfortably seated.

"I am a retired Postmaster living nearby with my wife and three sons in our ancestral house. My son, Shankara Sarma, is studying at Osmania Medical College and is a classmate of your daughter, Visalakshi. We have come to seek Visalakshi's hand in marriage for Shankara."

The family was taken aback by the unexpected proposal for Visalakshi. "With all due respect, how did you find our address, Sir?" Venkatachary sounded puzzled. The man appeared to be embarrassed by the question.

Our son is the class monitor and had to note down the addresses of all students to be submitted to the administrative office for updating. He saved Visala's address in the process," he answered, smiling sheepishly.

"Thank you very much for the proposal. Kindly give us some time to think about it," Venkatachary said, and the couple left shortly after.

Venkatachary inquired about Shankara Sarma's family through his friends. "Kasthuri, the boy's family, is highly educated and well-cultured, and the boy Shankara is intelligent and academically inclined like our Krishna," he said.

After a week of discussions and deliberations, the elders informed Visala about the proposal. She was initially taken aback but agreed without much resistance. It seemed to Kasthuri that Visala also nurtured a soft spot for the boy in her heart. It was then decided to proceed with the alliance.

Kasthuri withdrew her PF and gratuity funds to ensure her daughter's marriage was conducted in the best possible manner. There was no need to purchase any jewellery, as Kasthuri decided to hand over to her daughter whatever jewellery her mother had given her during her wedding. She had carefully preserved those over the years.

Kasthuri's siblings and aunt arrived in Hyderabad a week before the wedding. After many years, Kasthuri happily enjoyed every moment with them. There was so much to talk about, share, and tell each other. The wedding house became a centre of excitement, laughter, delicious food, and music.

Jalaja, Pankaja, and Kasthuri had stopped practising their music over the years and hardly sang anymore, much to Rathna's disappointment.

"Pankaja, Jalaja, Kasthuri! I want the three of you to resume singing again. What better occasion than our Vishu's wedding to do so?" Rathna opined.

The children also joined Rathna in persuading the three of them, and the stage was set for their concert a day before the wedding, following the Varamala ritual. Despite lacking regular practice, the three sisters melodiously performed beautiful *Thyagaraja and Muthu Swamy Deekshitar Krithis,* mesmerising both family and guests alike. The music program was the day's highlight, and Rathna took great pride in her role as their teacher.

The wedding ceremony of Kasthuri and Srinivasa's only daughter, Visalakshi, with Sankara Sarma concluded grandly. Soon after, Visalakshi left for her in-laws' house after bidding an emotional farewell to her family.

Chapter 20

Visala visited her family every other Sunday and was endlessly pampered by everyone. She happily shared stories about her life at her new home, and it was clear that she had settled in well and was content at her husband's house. Kasthuri felt relieved as a mother.

Visala and her classmate husband successfully passed the gruelling MBBS course. While Sankara topped Osmania Medical College that year, Visala secured a distinction, bringing great joy to both families.

One fine Sunday, Visala and Sankara came home with beaming faces. They seemed happy about something. "*Amma,* there is some good news that we have come to share with all of you," Visala said.

As everyone listened curiously, she continued, "Shankara and I had applied for a postgraduate program at a medical college in Birmingham, UK, and by God's grace, we have both been accepted by the college with full scholarships," Visala announced happily.

"Did you say the UK?" Krishna asked to confirm if he had heard it correctly.

"Yes, Krishna!" Shankara answered with a smile, and the entire family rejoiced at the news. They were pleased and proud of Visala and her husband.

"When are you both scheduled to leave?" Kasthuri asked.

"In a month," Sankara answered, and Kasthuri's heart sank.

"Just a month left!" exclaimed Kasthuri, and she rushed to the kitchen under the pretext of making a sweet dish to celebrate the good news. Alone in the kitchen, Kasthuri's eyes betrayed the tears she had held back with great difficulty. There were tears of joy and happiness, but at the same time, Kasthuri also shed a few tears of pain at the thought of parting from her only daughter. However, she regained her composure a few minutes later and walked into the living room with a tray of *Payasam* bowls.

Both sides of the family gave the young couple a heartfelt send-off, unaware of when they would see them again. Though it felt like a piece of her heart was being taken away, Kasthuri maintained a brave front and sent her daughter off with a smile. A couple of weeks after arriving in the UK, Visala wrote to her family that they had settled well on the University campus and that regular classes had begun, much to everyone's relief.

A few months later, Kasthuri received a marriage proposal for Krishna. The girl, Malathi, was the daughter of Ranganathan, an Upper Division clerk at Krishna's bank, who was very fond of Krishna. Malathi had graduated a couple of months ago with a degree in English literature. The alliance was fixed in no time, and Krishna married Malathi in a traditional

Iyengar ceremony. Malathi was a beautiful, extremely soft-spoken, good-natured girl everyone instantly liked.

Three years had passed swiftly. Krishna and Malathi were blessed with two children. The older one was a three-year-old girl named Divya. The younger one, a boy who had just turned one, was lovingly named Srinivasa Vasudev in memory of his grandfather. The two toddlers' innocent chatter and playful antics infused the house with vibrancy and happiness.

Meanwhile, Visala had completed her master's degree in gynaecology, and Shankara was now an orthopaedic surgeon. They began working as specialists at a local hospital in the UK. A few months later, the joyful news of Visala's pregnancy delighted both sides of the family.

However, a few weeks later, Visala's father-in-law passed away unexpectedly in Hyderabad. Since Visala had been advised against travelling by her doctor, Shankara made a quick trip to Hyderabad for his father's funeral. After all the rituals were complete, Shankara's mother accompanied him back to the UK. She was a great help to Visala during her pregnancy.

Visala and Shankara were blessed with a beautiful baby girl named Anupama. Visala regularly wrote to her mother and sent pictures of her little one. Kasthuri not only lovingly admired her granddaughter's photographs time and again but also proudly shared them with her colleagues at school. The baby girl had now turned two years old.

Days passed happily, and one evening, Krishna came home from the bank with a box of sweets. "*Peddayya,* I have been promoted as a senior officer and have been transferred to the bank's Bombay branch with immediate effect," he informed. While the family rejoiced at the news of his promotion, his transfer to Bombay was a surprise.

"We cannot allow you to live alone in a new place, Krishna. After looking for a suitable house, you could take Malathi and the children to be with you in Bombay," Venkatachary said.

"*Peddayya*, I wish to take *Amma* also with me to Bombay," Krishna said.

"That you wish to have your mother by your side wherever you go makes me happy and proud. If that's what Kasthuri too wishes, so be it," he said, looking at Kasthuri for her response.

"*Bavagaru*, with Visala away in the UK, I would be unable to be away from Krishna, too. I wish to go wherever my son goes," Kasthuri said. "However, it worries me that the three of you might feel lost and lonely while we are all gone." Kasthuri voiced her concern.

"Do not worry about us, child! Jagannath mentioned the last time he was here that he expected a transfer back to Hyderabad in a few months." Venkatachary assured, and the news of Jagannath's impending transfer to Hyderabad relieved Kasthuri and everyone else.

It was decided that Krishna would go to Bombay first. Kasthuri, Malathi, and the children would join him after Jagannath's family moved to Hyderabad. Additionally, Kasthuri needed to submit her resignation and serve her notice period at school.

Krishna left for Bombay within a couple of days, and the bank allocated him a spacious three-bedroom flat in a building in Colaba. His bank was located in the Fort area of Mumbai, and it would take him barely ten minutes to reach the office from home. Krishna couldn't wait for his mother and Malathi to see the lovely house. As expected, Jagannath returned to Hyderabad with his family. Krishna applied for a week's leave from the bank and came to Hyderabad to take his family to Bombay.

Meanwhile, Kasthuri's colleagues and other staff members organised a grand farewell for Kasthuri, which the entire family attended. In an emotional ceremony, she was honoured with a silk shawl, a sandalwood statue of the goddess Saraswati, and a memento. It was indeed a proud moment for the whole family. Kasthuri and Ramani promised each other they would stay in touch despite the distance.

Krishna had also made all the travel arrangements to take his mother, wife, and children to Bombay. The train to Bombay was scheduled to depart from Hyderabad at 6:00 a.m. Lakshmi had been crying incessantly; she loved Kasthuri immensely, and Kasthuri had been her pillar of strength during the most challenging circumstances. It pained her to part ways with Kasthuri, and the farewell was equally difficult for Kasthuri.

"*Peddayya*, I am as much your son as Jagannath *Anna*, and my house in Bombay is your house, too. Please visit Bombay whenever you wish to see us," Krishna's voice choked as he took leave of his uncle, who was more of a father figure to him. Krishna's emotional words moved Venkatachary to tears, and he embraced Krishna tightly.

Little Vasudev refused to leave Venkatachary at the railway station, wailing loudly as Krishna took the child from his grandfather's arms. As their family bid them an emotional farewell, Kasthuri, Krishna, Malathi, and the children boarded the train to Bombay with heavy hearts.

Chapter 21

The train arrived at Victoria Terminus railway station in Bombay around 9 am. As Kasthuri and her family alighted from the train, they were overwhelmed by the massive size of the station and the sea of people hurrying in and out. People travelling on the local trains crowded the platforms. Employees at BMC, LIC, and other offices near the VT station rushed out to avoid a late mark in the registers. Koli fisherwomen balancing large fish baskets to be sold in the markets outside the main gate, college students, textile workers, and shop owners all expertly manoeuvred their way out hastily.

As Kasthuri stood on the platform, looking at the rushing crowd in disbelief, Krishna urged his mother to move. "*Amma,* hold my hand and keep moving; otherwise, the crowd will push us aside." Kasthuri walked ahead, holding Krishna's hand and admiring the beautiful architecture of the Grand Victoria Terminus Station. It reminded Kasthuri of the grandeur of the Mysore Palace, and nostalgic memories of the Palace flooded back to her.

"*Amma,* we need to hurry." Krishna's voice brought her back to the present. Soon, the family stepped onto the bright, noisy street outside the station, vibrant and bustling with people. All the shops and eateries had already opened for the day's business, and the appetising aroma of sandwiches and masala chai filled the air. Electric trams ran on designated tracks around the station.

Krishna ushered his family toward a double-decker tram that came to a squealing stop just a few feet from where they stood. It was an enjoyable ride to Colaba, followed by a short walk from the tram stop to the *'Madhuban'* building, where Krishna had been allocated a 3-bedroom flat by his bank. As they walked, Kasthuri and Malathi marvelled at the numerous residential units built on top of each other in a single building, housing many families- a stark contrast to the large, independent houses in Tadipatri and Hyderabad.

As they walked up to the second floor of the building, Krishna showed them the door, which had the number 204. "This is our flat, our home," Krishna announced happily as he opened the door lock. Kasthuri and Malathi were both impressed by the well-ventilated, airy three-bedroom flat.

"How do you both like the house?" an excited Krishna asked.

"The house is quite lovely. However, it seems odd not to have open outdoor spaces connected to the house, and hence it feels somewhat constricted," Malathi remarked, to which Kasthuri agreed.

Kasthuri and Malathi, with Krishna's help, enthusiastically began setting up the house. They purchased new chairs for the living room, soft cotton mattresses for the bedrooms, and shiny brass and steel kitchenware. Kasthuri quickly stitched colourful curtains from old sarees for the windows. In just a few days, the two women transformed the flat into a lovely home.

It had already been a couple of months since the family moved to Bombay. Kasthuri and Malathi began to take a liking to the new city. Bombay was a lively place. Although the people were friendly, they were always on the move and very busy, unlike in Hyderabad, where people were laid-back and lethargic. While shopkeepers in Hyderabad typically open their shops after a leisurely breakfast around 10 am, shops in Bombay open as early as 6 am.

Kasthuri and Malathi were pleased with the abundance of fresh fruits and vegetables in the nearby markets.

While her mornings were quite busy helping Malathi prepare breakfast, getting the children ready, and packing lunch boxes for both the children and Krishna, Kasthuri enjoyed her time in the evenings. She would walk down to the beautiful Lakshmi Narayan temple to participate in the evening *bhajan* and *aarti* daily. From there, she would head to the nearby market to bring fresh vegetables and fruits for the next day.

Five happy years rolled by. Divya had turned eight and was promoted to the third grade. Little Vasu was now a bright six-year-old who attended first grade at a boys' school in Colaba. The family had settled well in Bombay by now. Not only the children but also Malathi and Kasthuri were able to converse fluently in Marathi and made good friends in their building and the neighbourhood.

One evening, while Kasthuri was returning from the market, she saw Manjari, the lady who sold *puri bhaji* and *vada pav*, on a cart outside their building. She was thrashing her young son while hurling abuse at him. The young lad was crying out in pain and pleading with his mother to stop. The young boy's plight, and she rushed toward them, dropping the vegetable bag she held to the ground.

"Manjari! *Kaay jhaale? Mulaala kaa maarat aahes?*", (Manjari, what happened? Why are you hitting the boy?) She asked as she tried to stop her.

"Kaki, tho punha parikshaat naapaas jhaala" (Kaki, he has failed again in his examination), she answered while trying to catch hold of the boy who hid behind Kasthuri.

"Thambva Manjari! (stop Manjari) mulaalaa maarne haa upaay naahi! (hitting the boy is not the solution).

"Mee kaay karu kasthuri kaki?", (What do I do?) Manjari collapsed onto the ground and began to cry.

Manjari was a single parent of two children, a boy and a girl, striving to make ends meet by working hard at her food cart. Her son, Abhijeet, had been struggling in the 8th grade for two consecutive years, which was a cause of great concern. She had been hoping and dreaming that her son would excel academically and one day ease her of financial burdens.

Kasthuri reassured Manjari that she would take Abhijeet home and talk to him to understand why he hadn't performed well on the exams. Manjari nodded and sat down on a nearby stool, wiping her tears with the edge of her sari.

Once home, Kasthuri comfortably seated Abhijeet and offered him a glass of Kokum Sharbat. After the child was a little relaxed, she spoke to him in detail about his school and the subjects he had been studying, while also trying to analyse the problems he was facing academically. She was amazed to find that Abhijeet was indeed a bright child. He had been performing reasonably well in all subjects except mathematics, in which he had been failing for the last two years.

"I need to help this child," Kasthuri had decided.

"Abhijeet, why don't you bring your mother along?" Kasthuri asked, and Abhijeet promptly ran down and returned shortly after with Manjari in tow.

"Manjari! Abhijeet is bright. However, he requires regular assistance and guidance to enhance his academic performance."

"But who will help him, Kasthuri *Kaki?* Paying the children's school fees is a daunting task. How can I afford to send him to special tuition?"

"You do not need to worry about fees. I shall help Abhijeet with his studies from now on," Kasthuri reassured her. Manjari folded her hands in gratitude, and her eyes welled up.

Later that evening, Kasthuri discussed the issue with Krishna, who appreciated her intention to help Abhijeet with his studies but was concerned that his mother shouldn't be stressing herself out.

"Do not worry, *Kanna.* I won't have to work too hard on Abhijeet. He only needs to get his basics right. An hour of guidance five days a week is enough to bring him back on track," Kasthuri reasoned, and Krishna reluctantly agreed.

Abhijeet was a sincere and hardworking boy, and in Kasthuri, he found an expert teacher, a guide, and a mentor all rolled into one. Ultimately, Kasthuri's time and efforts, combined with Abhijeet's diligence and dedication, paid off, and he not only passed his eighth grade with flying colours but also secured a centum in mathematics. Manjari and Abhijeet happily went to Kasthuri's house that evening with the report card and fruits. As Abhijeet and Manjari touched Kasthuri's feet and sought her blessings, Manjari's tears streamed down, completely wetting Kasthuri's feet.

Kasthuri continued to tutor Abhijeet throughout the next two years of high school. Abhijeet passed his SSC examination with eighty per cent. He secured a centum in mathematics, becoming one of the three students in Maharashtra to achieve this feat. Overjoyed, Abhijeet ran straight to Kasthuri's house to share the happy news, and an ecstatic Manjari followed him. Kasthuri was equally delighted and proud of her student.

"Abhijeet, Kasthuri *Aaji* was sure that you would do very well in your SSC examinations, and hence, she prepared *kheer* for you early in the morning itself," Malathi said as she handed over the bowls of *kheer* to Abhijeet and Manjari, who smiled at Kasthuri thankfully as they relished the sweet dish.

Krishna assisted Abhijeet with his admission to the prestigious Elphinstone College in the science stream, and his regular classes had begun. Kasthuri continued to support him not only in mathematics but also in other subjects. The combined efforts of the tutor and her student paid off, and Abhijeet not only excelled in his HSC examination but also gained admission to the Electrical and Electronics Engineering course at Victoria Technological University in Bombay. Needless to say, Kasthuri was elated.

"Thank you, God, for taking care of this lovely boy," Kasthuri said as she lit the lamps and said her prayers that evening, feeling happy and thankful.

Chapter 22

Malathi and Kasthuri sat in the living room, chatting after their afternoon lunch, when the postman handed them an envelope with UK stamps affixed to it. "Malathi, it seems to be a letter from Vishu," said an excited Kasthuri as she hurriedly tore open the envelope. The letter brought the happy news that Visala was coming to Bombay with her husband and daughter for a two-month-long vacation; needless to say, Kasthuri was overjoyed. It had been almost five years since she had seen her daughter and held her in her arms.

Visala would regularly write to her mother and send their photographs, but a void in Kasthuri's heart couldn't be filled. Visala and her husband were financially well-off and highly sought-after doctors in the UK; however, their hectic schedules prevented them from travelling to India often.

On the day of Visala's arrival, Kasthuri and her family arrived at the airport half an hour before Visala's flight landed. *"Amma,* there comes our Vishu," Krishna shouted in happy excitement as he pointed to a pretty woman dressed in trousers and a long polka-dotted shirt with a scarf stylishly wrapped around her neck, walking out of the airport alongside her husband and teenage daughter. Kasthuri removed her spectacles, wiped them clean with the edge of her sari, and put them on again to clearly see her daughter. There she was! Her Vishu! She waved to them as she ran toward them, with Shankara and Anupama following closely behind, beaming excitedly.

"*Amma,*" Vishu squealed in delight as she hugged Kasthuri tightly. Kasthuri fondly touched her daughter's face and shoulders, studying her closely. Gone was the chubby, pretty Visala with long, lustrous hair. Visala was now slim, wore spectacles, and sported short hair. "Why did you chop off your hair, Vishu, and why are you wearing spectacles?" Kasthuri asked as she touched her daughter's short hair.

"*Amma,* with my job, it's been difficult to maintain long hair, so I cut it short," Visala explained sheepishly, aware that her mother was unhappy with her short hair. Anupama, now a beautiful teenager, ran into her grandmother's loving arms.

Once home, at lunch, Visala was delighted to see that her mother and sister-in-law had painstakingly prepared all of her and Shankar's favourite dishes. "It's been so long since I ate such delicious food, *Amma!*" Visala said as she happily ate the food to her heart's content. The scene melted Kasthuri's heart. Once lunch was finished and everyone had retired for a small afternoon nap, Visalakshi rested her head on her mother's lap. As Kasthuri lovingly ran her fingers through her hair, Visala started to cry softly. "What is it, my child? Why do you cry?" asked an alarmed Kasthuri.

"Nothing, *Amma!* Just that I missed you immensely," Visala said. Kasthuri's eyes welled up as she lovingly kissed her daughter's forehead.

It was nothing short of a festive atmosphere in the house for the next few weeks. Krishna would come home early to spend time with his family. Unending chats and conversations took place over piping hot, delicious food. Kasthuri would lovingly cook and treat Visala and her family to lip-smacking Maharashtrian delicacies, such as *Thali Peeth, Kothimbir Vadi, Bharli Vangi, and Puran Poli,* which they thoroughly enjoyed.

"You seem to have mastered the Maharashtrian cuisine, *Ammamma,*" Anupama complimented as she savoured a spoonful of the delicious Sabudana Khichdi.

"Not only the cuisine, Anu! Your Ammamma has also mastered the Marathi language! She now speaks Marathi better than the locals," Krishna revealed as Visala and Shankara looked at Kasthuri with admiration. During the evenings, the family would head to Marine Drive, spend time at the promenade, and relish fresh and spicy *bhelpuri.*

Every time Visala's family flew to Bombay, she never failed to make a short trip to Hyderabad to meet her uncle, aunt, and cousins. Her mother and her brother's family would join her, too. This time, the entire family visited Hyderabad and returned to Bombay after spending a few happy days there. A couple of days after they returned to Bombay, Kasthuri received a letter from Rathna expressing her wish to see Visala. She had planned to travel to Bombay along with Bhagwan.

A week later, Rathna arrived with Bhagwan in tow. While her dear aunt's arrival made Kasthuri extremely happy, it saddened her to see Rathna limping and walking with great difficulty. Rathna had fallen in her house a few weeks ago. Though the pain had reduced, she had not fully recovered. As

Kasthuri chatted with Bhagwan and her aunt that night, she expressed concern about Rathna staying alone in Sakleshpur in this condition.

"*Chikkamma*, I can no longer allow you to stay alone in Sakleshpur. It is time for you to shift to Bombay." Although Rathna resisted initially, she eventually agreed after Kasthuri and Krishna strongly insisted.

"But what about the house in Sakleshpur?" Ratha voiced her concern.

"Do not worry about it, *Chikkamma*! I shall first shift all your things to Bombay and later arrange for the house sale, too," Bhagwan assured Rathna, and Rathna was relieved. Thus, it was decided that Rathna would not return to Sakleshpur but would stay with Kasthuri and her family in Bombay, a decision welcomed by all.

Visalakshi spent another happy month with her family in Bombay, but like all good times, her vacation ended quickly. It was time for Visalakshi and her family to leave for the UK. "I shall come back soon, *Amma*, probably in a couple of years," Visala promised Kasthuri before leaving. It broke her heart to see her family waving at her sadly as she walked into the airport. Nevertheless, she boarded the flight to the UK, carrying many beautiful memories in her heart and a determination to visit India soon.

Kasthuri and the others returned from the airport to a home that suddenly felt empty and dull.

Chapter 23

Nine more years rolled by, and a lot changed during that time. Although Rathna had recovered after moving to Bombay and was doing reasonably well, she passed away peacefully in her sleep about three years later. A few years ago, Venkatachary passed away due to age-related complications, and Lakshmi also followed her husband in death a year later.

"A generation of righteous and selfless people has ended," Kasthuri would tell Krishna and Malathi.

Kasthuri had turned 65 that year, and she had maintained good health due to the grace of God. The 48-year-old Krishna was doing exceptionally well and had been promoted to the bank's general manager position. He had also been allocated a four-bedroom flat in the same building, which Kasthuri and Malathi had tastefully decorated.

Divya was now a 22-year-old, beautiful, and bright young woman in her fourth and final year of the chemical engineering course at Victoria Technological Institute, popularly known as VJT in Bombay, while her younger brother, Vasu, was in his second year of the electrical and electronics course at the same college.

Visala and Shankara continued practising as doctors and were happily settled in Birmingham. The 21-year-old Anupama was now pursuing her pre-medical course at King's College in London.

Anupama was fond of her grandmother and would call Kasthuri every Sunday morning. She spoke with her about her course, college, and friends. During one such conversation, Anu mentioned to Kasthuri a 58-year-old man named George, who was studying with her and was her classmate.

"Is he not too old to pursue a medical degree, Anu?" Kasthuri seemed surprised.

"Age is just a number, *Ammamma*. He is more passionate and enthusiastic about the course than most of us in class."

After her conversation with Anu, Kasthuri sat in the living room, reflecting on Anu's classmate George and admiring his determination. "Did I give up on my dream too easily?" she asked herself.

"Age is just a number, *Ammamma!*" Anu's words kept echoing in her head. Kasthuri did not realise how long she had sat there, lost in deep thought, until she felt Malathi's hand on her shoulder. "Is anything the matter, *Athe*? You do not seem alright."

"Nothing at all, Malathi!" Kasthuri replied, and the two women walked to the dining table for lunch. For the next two days, Kasthuri did not seem like herself.

"*Athe* seems to be bothered by something. She hasn't been eating properly since yesterday." Malathi expressed her concern to her husband that evening.

"*Amma*, are you feeling unwell?" Krishna asked his mother.

"I'm doing fine, *Kanna*, don't worry!" Kasthuri answered as she retreated to her room early that night after dinner, leaving Krishna and his wife puzzled. She kept tossing and turning in bed that night as sleep eluded her. By early the next morning, she had made up her mind and decided to speak to her son about a decision she had reached. After bathing and saying her daily prayers, she entered the living room. Since it was Sunday, Krishna seemed relaxed, reading the newspaper and enjoying his hot filter coffee.

"*Kanna*! I wish to speak with you," Kasthuri said, clearing her throat.

"What is it, *Amma?*"

"Long ago, while I was in school, I made a promise to my father that I was unfortunately unable to fulfil, and the thought has been bothering me ever since, more so in the last few days."

"What was the promise about, *Amma?*" asked Krishna with inquisitiveness.

"It had been my father's wish that I study well and become a graduate, and eventually, fulfilling his wish and making him proud became my only dream and goal."

"How is it that you never mentioned it to me, *Amma*? " Krishna seemed surprised as he set the newspaper aside and listened to his mother with full attention.

"Over the years, I had forgotten about it myself!"

"*Amma*, do not worry! If *Thatha* were alive today, he would be immensely proud of what you have achieved. You have retired as a respected assistant headmistress of Government High School and raised us well."

"I understand, *Kanna*! Yet, I want to pursue the dream I have kept hidden in my heart for so long." Kasthuri felt resolute, and the spark of learning within her reignited, glowing brightly once more.

"Why now, *Amma?*"

"If not now, when, *Kanna*? I am not getting any younger. The sooner I start, the better it is."

"*Amma!* You have endured many hardships and worked tirelessly day and night to provide Vishu and me with a good life. It is my turn now. I want you to be happy and lead a relaxed life."

"You have been taking care of me well, Krishna. However, returning to my studies will bring me happiness at this point in my life. Please do not refuse." Meanwhile, Malathi and the children gathered in the living room. They sat there listening to the conversation between the mother and son.

"*Amma*, you might not be able to handle all that academic stress at this age. I do not want you to risk your health over a childhood dream. Please reconsider your decision."

"I promise to take care of my health, Krishna! Please let me live my dream!" Kasthuri choked out, her voice trembling. The children and Malathi rushed to Kasthuri and tried to console her.

"Amma! I cannot bear to see you so sad. If going back to your studies is what would make you happy, so be it," Krishna said as he walked up to his mother and kissed her forehead.

The conversation was interrupted by the ringing of the doorbell. As Vasu opened the door, Abhijeet and his wife, Suchitra, walked in. "We had come out for our morning walk. Suchi wanted to see *Kaki*, so we stopped by," said Abhijeet as he and Suchi sat down on the chairs near Kasthuri.

Abhijeet was now an engineer at Godrej, married to the lovely Suchitra, a mathematics postgraduate. She had worked as a lecturer at St. Xavier's College. The couple was blessed with a four-year-old son. Abhijeet made it a point to visit Kasthuri's home at least once a week to spend time with Kasthuri and her family. Suchitra was equally fond of Kasthuri and would gladly join him.

Over a delicious breakfast of soft, fluffy *dosas* and coconut *chutney,* Krishna informed Abhijeet of Kasthuri's interest in pursuing her dream of graduating. Although the unexpected news initially took Abhijeet aback, he wholeheartedly appreciated Kasthuri, as did Suchitra. "Kasthuri *Kaki*! It is commendable that you still have the zeal to pursue your education even at this age. Kudos to you!" Suchi said.

"Avva, could you travel to college and attend regular classes daily?" Divya asked Kasthuri.

The question made Kasthuri think, and before she could answer, Krishna firmly voiced his concern: "*Amma*, I don't think it's wise to put yourself through the rigorous regime of everyday travel to and from college and to sit through long hours at college every day at this age." Kasthuri nodded halfheartedly, and after a few moments of silence, Suchitra made a suggestion that appealed to everyone.

"Krishna *mama*! The Bombay Open University holds on-campus classes twice a week for students. Meanwhile, its library is open to students every day."

"Perfect!" Krishna exclaimed, and Kasthuri beamed with joy.

"However, I'm not sure if the application forms are still being given out," Suchitra was doubtful. Luckily, applications for the BSc in Mathematics were being accepted at the University. Kasthuri soon enrolled in the first-year B.Sc. mathematics course at the Bombay Open University, and all the relevant textbooks were purchased. Kasthuri's joy knew no bounds, and she treated her family to delicious ice cream on the way home from the University.

Once in her room after lunch, Kasthuri sat on her cot and took her textbooks one by one from the cloth bag, touching them lovingly. There was a month left before the course started, but Kasthuri couldn't wait to begin solving complicated mathematical problems. She went through her books and realised that most concepts were newly introduced at the B.Sc. level and required a higher level of understanding. She might need some help with these.

When Abhijeet and Suchitra came by a week later, Kasthuri was in the living room, trying to solve a few Algebra problems. She looked up at them with a smile. Vasu told the couple, "*Avva* has been happily lost in the world of her books and has been oblivious to anything else."

"Already, *Kaki?* Please let me know if I can help," Suchi graciously offered.

"Thank you so much, Suchi! I'm certain I will need all the support," Kasthuri said, smiling.

"*Kaki*, I'm free now since the college is closed for summer vacation. Shall we spend a couple of hours each day covering a few topics from your textbooks for a month before your classes at the campus kick off?"

"Sure, Suchi!" Kasthuri answered with childlike excitement. It was decided that Suchi would come home every evening between 4 pm and 6 pm to help Kasthuri with her studies. "Let's start with our first class tomorrow, *Kaki!*" Suchi was equally excited, to which Kasthuri nodded with a broad smile and a twinkle in her eyes.

"Beware, *Kaki*! Your teacher has a reputation for being strict and ruthless with her students. Don't say I didn't warn you earlier!" Abhijeet joked.

"I am sure my teacher is considerate enough with her older students. Right, Suchi?"

"Of course, *Kaki!*" Suchi answered, laughing aloud, and everyone else joined in. The clock struck 7 pm, interrupting the joyous laughter, and the couple slowly got up to leave.

The next evening, at 4 pm, the doorbell rang. Kasthuri, sitting in the living room and waiting for Suchitra, sprang to her feet to open the door. In walked a smiling Suchitra. Kasthuri led her into her room, where she had arranged all her textbooks neatly on a wooden table that Krishna had moved in the previous night. He had also placed a couple of wooden chairs so Kasthuri and Suchitra could sit comfortably by the table.

As they sat, Suchitra asked, "Which is your favourite math subject, *Kaki?*"

"Algebra," came the reply.

"Let's start with Algebra, then!" she said, and soon, the two of them delved deep into the magical world of mathematics, only to be brought back to the present as Malathi called out to them, holding a couple of shiny brass tumblers of piping hot, aromatic filter coffee. Kasthuri took the coffee tumbler and glanced at the wall clock, which indicated 6:15 pm.

"Oh my God! It is already past 6 pm. You are such a good teacher, Suchi! I was so engrossed in your class that I didn't realise the time," Kasthuri remarked.

In a month, Suchi covered several vital topics in algebra and solid geometry. That evening, Krishna walked in just as Suchitra and Kasthuri had wrapped up their class. The two of them and Malathi sat in the living room happily chatting as they enjoyed tumblers of hot tea while munching on some delicious chivda.

"Well! Well! May I beg to join you, lovely ladies, in this tea party?" Krishna quipped dramatically as the three women laughed, while Malathi walked into the kitchen to fetch a cup of tea for her husband.

"*Amma* seems to enjoy your classes, Suchi! She eagerly looks forward to these study sessions with you every day. Thank you for taking the time off to help *Amma*," Krishna said in an appreciative tone, while Kasthuri nodded in approval.

"Do not be so formal, Krishna *Mama!* It's my absolute pleasure. *Kaki's* enthusiasm and zeal to learn are inspiring, and I'm learning with her, too."

"*Amma*! Your first campus class will begin the day after tomorrow, and so will your student life," Krishna gave the good news.

"The day after tomorrow?" Kasthuri said in a tone of excitement and disbelief.

"Yes! You heard it right, *Amma*!" His mother's excitement made Krishna happy. Malathi and Suchi, too, rejoiced at the news.

"Krishna *Mama!* My college starts the day after tomorrow and ends at 3 pm every day. Before heading home, I can come straight here from college and spend a couple of hours with Kasthuri *Kaki* every day."

"Coming here straight from your college daily might be tiresome for you, Suchi! Wouldn't it?"

"Krishna is right, Suchi! Also, I wouldn't want you to keep little Rohan waiting for you every single day." Kasthuri said.

"Do not worry, *Kaki*. Rohan takes a nap in the afternoon anyway. Moreover, I don't need to worry about Rohan, as my mother-in-law takes good care of him."

"Suchi! Amma would have to attend campus classes on Mondays and Saturdays from 10 am to 3 pm; hence, she would be left with only four days a week," Krishna said, thinking for a while.

He then devised a plan and discussed it with Suchi and Kasthuri. It was decided that Suchitra would come down on Tuesdays and Thursdays to assist Kasthuri. Meanwhile, Krishna would take care of his mother's studies for a couple of hours after he returned home from the office on Wednesdays and Fridays.

"In that case, I would happily help *Kaki* with Algebra, Solid Geometry, and Trigonometry. Would you like to take Calculus, Probability, and Statistics, Krishna *Mama*?" Suchitra asked.

"So be it," answered Krishna. The two teachers decided to give their students a day off on Sundays. The plan appealed to everyone; needless to say, Kasthuri was the happiest.

Chapter 24

It was a bright Monday morning, and classes at the University were set to begin that day. Kasthuri woke up at dawn and bathed early. With spring in her step and a song on her lips, she went about her daily chores. After a hearty breakfast and a tumbler full of hot filter coffee, Kasthuri walked into her room to get ready. She wore her favourite lavender-colored *Venkatagiri* cotton saree, featuring a broad zari border, and a matching blouse. She styled her hair neatly into a tight bun. A simple gold chain and a couple of gold bangles completed her look.

"*Amma*! Are you ready? We must start now to avoid delay on the first day," Krishna hurried. Kasthuri walked out of the room holding a cotton bag that contained a notebook, a pencil box, and a geometry box.

"Here, *Athe,* I have packed *chapati* and lady's finger curry for lunch," Malathi said as she handed a small wire basket to Kasthuri. Kasthuri lovingly touched her cheek. Vasu and Divya walked with Kasthuri to the car to see her off. As their vehicle entered the vast, lush green campus of Bombay University, Kasthuri's heart missed a beat. Kasthuri and Krishna were guided toward a classroom on the ground floor.

"*Amma*! Take care! I shall send the office driver to pick you up at the gate in the afternoon," Krishna said after leaving Kasthuri outside her classroom before heading to work. Kasthuri's heart pounded with excitement, and she felt butterflies in her stomach as she entered the classroom. Approximately twenty-five students were already seated in the classroom. The students mistook Kasthuri for one of the teachers and stood up to greet her.

"Please sit down. I am a student too, just like all of you," she said with a smile as she walked towards the seating area, much to the disbelief of her classmates. Kasthuri smiled at the pretty young girl sitting on the first bench as she made herself comfortable in the seat next to her.

In about five minutes, Prof. Suhasini, the head of the mathematics department, walked in. Kasthuri and the other students stood up to greet her. Prof. Suhasini was a short, stout, cheerful-looking lady in her early fifties. She introduced herself and asked the students to introduce themselves, too, one by one. It was now Kasthuri's turn to introduce herself. "I am Kasthuri. I am a sixty-five-year-old retired assistant school headmistress and a proud grandmother to two lovely grandchildren."

"Out of sheer respect and curiosity, may I ask what made you take up this course at this age, Madam Kasthuri?"

"It has always been my wish to complete my graduation, and I have tried several times earlier to pursue my education, but unfortunately, I couldn't succeed. I guess the time is right now," Kasthuri explained with a smile.

"It is indeed laudable that at an age when people are ready to hang up their shoes and relax, you have chosen to pursue your dream. Kudos to you, Madam," Professor Suhasini said as she stood up and clapped in appreciation. The rest of the students followed suit and clapped enthusiastically for Kasthuri and her determination to pursue her graduation.

Professor Suhasini began with a one-hour introduction class to Calculus. After a 15-minute break, Prof. Balakrishna introduced the fundamental algebraic concepts of Integers and Divisibility. Students were then given several problems from both topics and asked to solve them in the following hour. Both teachers made their classes engaging and interactive. The bell ringing at 1 pm signalled the start of the lunch break, which would last for an hour.

Prajakta More, the 19-year-old girl sitting next to Kasthuri, turned to her with a smile and asked, "Madam! You remind me so much of my grandmother. Can I call you *Aaji?*"

"Yes, of course, dear! You remind me of my granddaughter, Divya. She is a couple of years older than you," Kasthuri answered affectionately.

"*Aaji,* shall we sit on the lawn outside and have lunch?" Prajakta asked. Kasthuri nodded, and the two walked towards the beautifully landscaped lawn, choosing a spot under the shade of a temple tree that occasionally dropped lovely, white, fragrant flowers. They were just about to eat when a girl from the same class approached them. "May I join you both?" she asked, to which Kasthuri and Prajakta readily agreed.

The twenty-five-year-old Aarti Keskar was a widowed single mother living with her parents and little daughter. After graduating, she hoped to secure a job to support herself. As they all sat together for lunch, slowly chatting and getting to know each other, a young boy from their class, sitting alone on a stone bench away from everyone, caught Kasthuri's attention. While everyone else ate, he sat on the bench reading a novel.

"Prajakta, could you please walk up and call that boy to join us?" Kasthuri requested Prajakta. When the boy walked toward them with Prajakta, looking puzzled, Kasthuri invited him to join them.

"Oh no, no, Madam. That's okay. I am not hungry!" the boy hesitated.

"I am as old as your grandmother. Won't you listen to me? We have brought enough food that can be shared," Kasthuri insisted. The other two girls also requested him to join them. "Thank you," Akash said as he sat down with them and thoroughly enjoyed the food they shared with him.

Akash Rane was a bright, jovial, and energetic young man who worked as a cashier at a pharmacy to support his low-income family. Luckily for him, his employer allowed him a half-day of leave twice a week to attend classes on campus, although this came with a cut in salary. Kasthuri instantly liked the lovable, hardworking boy. "I must remember to pack an extra lunchbox for Akash from the next class," she thought.

Kasthuri thoroughly enjoyed and looked forward to her campus classes. All the teachers and students developed a great liking and immense respect for Kasthuri. While all her fellow students lovingly called her *Aaji*, her teachers respectfully addressed her as 'Kasthuri Madam'. They were amazed by her ability to grasp the subject quickly and her dedication and sincerity toward her studies, even at sixty-five.

Though Kasthuri shared a warm relationship with all her classmates, she particularly liked Prajakta, Akash, and Aarti. She loved spending time with the bubbly youngsters and exploring the beautiful University campus. They would sometimes enjoy a plate of hot *Batata Vadas* and *Onion Bhajis* from the campus canteen and, at other times, walk a few blocks to savour a glass of refreshing sugarcane juice. Kasthuri started to enjoy the student life she had longed for. The University had an excellent, well-stocked library. Kasthuri loved spending time here after classes, looking for new books to borrow and read at home.

Aside from her classes on campus, Suchitra and Krishna regularly assisted her with her studies at home. At times, she would tackle new, complex concepts independently, which pleasantly surprised her son. "*Amma*! If only you had pursued your education, you would be a name to reckon with in the field of mathematics," he appreciated.

While she worked hard throughout the week, Malathi and Krishna ensured she wouldn't touch her books on Sundays. That day, she relaxed and enjoyed quality time with her family. Months rolled by, and Kasthuri performed outstandingly in her examinations, passing her first year with upper distinction. While Akash and Aarti also secured distinctions in their exams, Prajakta achieved a first-class result. Nevertheless, the friends were all happy.

Aarti invited the three of them to her home for lunch the next day to celebrate her daughter's birthday and their success in the exams. When Kasthuri hesitated, Aarti insisted, "*Aaji*, it would mean a lot to me if you could come. I would love you to meet my daughter and parents. You could also bring Divya and Vasu along. We would all love to meet them."

Divya and Vasu agreed to accompany Kasthuri to Aarti's house the following Sunday. Aarti's three-year-old daughter was as cute as a doll and played happily with everyone. Kasthuri bought her a tiny gold ring, which she was delighted to wear on her little finger. Aarti's parents were also gracious hosts and were pleased to meet Kasthuri and the others.

A sumptuous, vegetarian Maharashtrian lunch was arranged, which Kasthuri and all the others thoroughly enjoyed. Not only Kasthuri but also Divya and Vasu had a great time with her grandmother's friends and Aarti's baby.

Another year passed, and Kasthuri achieved top marks in her second year. After a two-month break, classes resumed, marking the beginning of her third and final year.

As usual, Krishna dropped Kasthuri off at the University that day. Aarti, Prajakta, and Akash waited for her at the classroom door. Kasthuri was suddenly reminded of her childhood friend Juliet, who would wait for her at school. Her eyes welled up at the memory of Juliet. She approached her friends while wiping her eyes, and the four of them walked in together.

The difficulty level increased in the third year compared to the previous two years. There were many more subjects.

"Suchi, with the number of new subjects that have been added to the syllabus this year, it seems that I need to work much harder this year," Kasthuri remarked.

"Relax, *Aaji!* You have been working hard every year. We both need to sit with Krishna *Mama* and make a study plan. If we approach the syllabus methodically, things will become easy," Suchi opined.

A study plan was thereby chalked out. According to the plan, the entire syllabus would be comfortably completed two months before the examinations, allowing Kasthuri ample time to revise it. Now that things were under control and a proper plan had been made, Kasthuri felt relaxed and at peace.

Days passed. Kasthuri, with the help of her mentors, not only finished the entire syllabus but also spent a month revising all her subjects. With a month left before the final examinations began, the University announced a study leave for that month. Kasthuri and her friends wished each other good luck and parted, but not before enjoying plates of spicy Vada pav at the canteen.

A few days passed, and Kasthuri felt too weak that morning to get out of bed. When she tried to wake up, Kasthuri felt her head spinning. "A glass of lemon water would probably make me feel better," she thought. Kasthuri got up with great difficulty and slowly walked out of her room. Just as she entered the living room, she experienced a blackout and fell to the ground. Sitting in the living room reading the morning newspaper, Krishna sprang to his feet and held his mother.

"Malathi! Vasu! Divya!" he screamed. Malathi and the children came running, shocked to see Kasthuri lying unconscious in Krishna's arms. Malathi ran into the kitchen to get a glass of water while Krishna and the children tried to wake Kasthuri. As Malathi sprinkled a little water on her face, Kasthuri opened her eyes slowly.

"Amma, what happened? How did you fall?" Krishna asked frantically. Kasthuri signalled with her thumb, pointing toward her mouth as if she needed water. Krishna slowly helped her sip water from the glass, and after a while, she sat up, still feeling weak. *"Amma,* would you like to sleep?" Krishna asked, to which Kasthuri nodded in the affirmative. Krishna and Vasu assisted Kasthuri in standing slowly, walked her to her bed, and helped her lie down.

"Vasu, why don't you run downstairs to Dr. Sawant's flat and ask him to rush up to see *Amma?*" Dr. Nilesh Sawant arrived within a few minutes, still in his night suit, carrying his stethoscope and emergency medical kit in his hand. After thoroughly checking Kasthuri, he informed Krishna that it was a classic case of exhaustion and dehydration. "She needs to be on complete bed rest for at least a week, and I shall put her on intravenous fluids and electrolytes," he advised.

"Would you be prescribing any medicines?" Krishna asked.

"Just some Multivitamins and Iron capsules. Nothing else," the doctor answered as he inserted a needle into her vein to fix the cannula for administering intravenous fluids and electrolytes. "After a couple of hours, I shall send my nurse to change the bottle. In the meantime, you can give her a non-oily breakfast and some fruit juice.

Malathi quickly served soft *idlis* with zero-spice coconut *chutney*. Krishna gently helped Kasthuri sit up to eat breakfast. A little later, Malathi brought her a glass of freshly squeezed *Mousambi* juice. A tired Kasthuri gradually drifted off to sleep. About two hours later, Dr. Sawant's nurse arrived to replace the empty intravenous bottle with a new one. By afternoon, Kasthuri began to feel better.

"Krishna, I feel as though my energy is slowly returning to me," she said with a smile.

"*Amma*, you scared us. Despite my pleas, you haven't rested well over the last two weeks. You were studying and working hard, even on Sundays. The doctor says you have exhausted yourself," Krishna sounded worried.

"Don't worry, *Kanna*! I will be all right in a day or two," Kasthuri reassured her son.

"Doctor Sawant has advised you to rest for a complete week. If I see you getting out of that bed for a week, I will be really upset, *Amma*!" Krishna lovingly warned his mother, to which Kasthuri nodded with a smile.

Under the loving care of her family, Kasthuri recovered well within a week and was back on her feet. Krishna was happy to see his mother fit and active. However, with the exams approaching in a month, he knew his mother would insist on studying hard again, which made him anxious about her health. As expected, Kasthuri brought up the topic that morning while they ate breakfast.

"Kanna, with less than a month left for the exams, I was just wondering if I could start revising from today!"

"*Amma,* you have barely recovered. Your syllabus is over, and you have already revised for a full month. I want you to take it easy now, at least for another week". Kasthuri understood her son's concern but felt disappointed. When Suchi came to see her that evening, Kasthuri told her of Krishna's ultimatum.

"Krishna *mama* is right in not letting you exert yourself, Kaki. Your health is of utmost importance to us all. Anyway, you have thoroughly revised the entire syllabus once. What then is your worry, Kaki?"

"I need to work more on real analysis and number theory. I do not feel very confident about those, " Kasthuri admitted.

"*Kaki,* it's just your feeling. You have prepared really well. Trust me," Suchi tried to reassure Kasthuri. A week passed, and Kasthuri felt perfectly fine. The complete rest helped her get back on her feet.

"*Kanna,* I just have two more weeks for the examinations. Shall I start revising a little now?" Kasthuri asked her son.

"*Amma,* I understand your desire to excel in your exams. But your health and wellbeing are all that matter to me. Please promise me you won't strain yourself too much. You must rest well for a few hours in the afternoons and go to bed early at night."

"I promise, *Kanna,*" Kasthuri said as she hurried to her room, delighted to be reunited with her books.

The day of the first examination had finally arrived. Suchi and Abhijeet also came by to wish Kasthuri the best on their way to work. Malathi packed a box with biscuits, a bottle of plain water, and a bottle of buttermilk. "Do not forget to keep yourself hydrated, Athe. Have sips of water and buttermilk throughout the exam," she gently reminded Kasthuri.

"I will, dear!" Kasthuri answered, lovingly patting Malathi's cheek as she walked into her room and stood before the photo frame of her father. "*Appa,* I need all your blessings now more than anything else. Help me complete all my examinations well," she prayed, folding her hands.

She opened her wardrobe, pulled out a drawer, and retrieved a wooden box. Inside the box was the Stewart Conway pen that Sir Albert had gifted her. She looked at the pen lovingly and carefully placed it in her geometry box. She had filled the pen with ink, changed the nib, and prepared it the previous day. She planned to use that pen for all her final-year degree exams.

"*Amma!* Time to go!" Krishna's voice broke the silence, and Kasthuri hurried into the living room with her bag. Malathi and the children accompanied Kasthuri to the car, wished her good luck, and waved until the vehicle disappeared around the curve of the road.

Chapter 25

It was the day of her last exam, and Kasthuri finished writing her favourite and easiest paper, Linear Algebra, much earlier than the stipulated time. She checked and rechecked her calculations before submitting her paper and leaving the examination hall, feeling as light as a feather.

Kasthuri wanted to dance her heart out as she walked through the corridors toward the lawn. However, she managed to control that urge and sat under her favourite temple tree. She gathered the fresh flowers in her palms. As she inhaled their divine fragrance, Kasthuri was suddenly reminded of the flowers her father would offer the deities at their home in Sakleshpur. The memory of Sakleshpur filled her heart with fond recollections of her childhood.

The ringing of the shrill bell brought her back to the present, and soon, her friends walked up to her, beaming happily. "*Aaji*, why don't we go out for a quick lunch today to celebrate the completion of the final exam of our final year? " Akash suggested, with excitement written all over his face.

"And yes, it is going to be my treat. I received my bonus just yesterday." Akash added.

"I am glad you have received your bonus, *mulaa*! But that doesn't mean you will blow it all in one day," Kasthuri chided lovingly. "We shall all share the cost equally!"

"*Aaji*, please! I insist! It would mean a lot to me." Akash was persistent. Kasthuri and others had no choice but to agree.

"Let me check with Krishna to see if we can keep the car and the driver with us until we finish our lunch," Kasthuri said, and they all walked up to the office to call Krishna on the phone.

Fortunately for them, Krishna was okay with letting them keep the car for as long as they wanted. The four of them happily walked toward the car, and Akash directed the driver to *Pancham Puriwala,* located near the Fort area. "*Aaji*, I chose this restaurant because it's purely vegetarian and because they serve delicious food," Akash explained.

The hotel seemed modest, but as Akash mentioned, the *Palak puris* and *Masala puris*, along with their famous aloo ki sabzi, tasted heavenly. "This is the tastiest *lassi* we have ever tasted," opined the three ladies as they savoured the cool, sweet *lassi* topped with fresh *Malai*. They thoroughly enjoyed the lunch and thanked Akash profusely for the hearty treat.

After lunch, Akash, Aarti, and Prajakta walked Kasthuri to the car and, after assuring her that they would come home soon to meet her, headed together toward the local train station. Kasthuri's eyes blurred with tears as her dear friends moved farther away. She had already begun to miss them. When Kasthuri reached home, Malathi warmly welcomed her with a bowl of her favourite *Gasagase Payasa.*

"How did the last exam go, *Athe?*". Malathi enquired.

"Very well, Malathi," Kasthuri answered. After briefly chatting with her daughter-in-law, she entered her room to freshen up and rest. Kasthuri did not realise how long she had slept until Krishna's voice woke her. He was speaking to Malathi and the children. Kasthuri slowly woke and walked into the living room.

"Here comes Smt. Kasthuri Srinivasa, B.Sc. in Mathematics, "Vasu announced dramatically, making Kasthuri laugh heartily. "Oh my God! It is 7 pm already. I didn't realise I slept for so long," Kasthuri remarked as she glanced at the wall clock.

"*Amma*, the exams are finally over, and you will be free from tomorrow. No more studies, no more working out the problems, and no more memorising the formulae. How does it make you feel?" Krishna asked.

"I shall miss my classes, books, friends, teachers, and, of course, the study sessions with you and Suchi immensely," she admitted with a smile.

A month passed, and the much-awaited B.Sc. The results were to be announced by 10 am the following morning. Krishna and Vasu went to the University to check the results. In the meantime, the entire family, including Abhijeet and Suchitra, gathered in the living room, waiting for the father-son duo to return home with good news.

"You have passed, *Avva*," Vasu announced with a straight face upon reaching home.

"Just passed?" Kasthuri asked, but the two did not answer. As the tension built, a few seconds later, they shouted together excitedly, "We have the University topper here with us."

"What!" asked Kasthuri in disbelief.

"You have heard it right, *Amma*! You are the topper in B.Sc. Mathematics at the Bombay Open University this year!" Krishna continued to scream in excitement as he hugged his mother tightly.

"We are all so very proud of you, *Amma*. Your journey has been truly inspiring." Krishna was overwhelmed, and so was the rest of the family. Malathi had happy tears and looked at her mother-in-law with immense pride and love. The children's happiness knew no bounds as they held Kasthuri's hands and started to dance with her. An ecstatic Suchi joined in, too, and so did Abhijeet. "Well done, *Kaki*. I feel the proudest today," Suchi said as she held Kasthuri close and kissed her cheek.

Kasthuri, too, was overwhelmed with mixed emotions. She held both Suchi and Krishna lovingly on either side and said, "How can I thank you both? If it hadn't been for the two of you, I wouldn't have achieved this success." Tears began to pour out of her eyes as Suchi, Krishna, and the rest of the family cheered and comforted her. "Give me a minute," she said as she entered her room. A short while later, Kasthuri emerged from her room with two bags.

"Here, dear, this is for you," she said as she handed Suchi a cover.

"What is this, *Kaki*?" Suchi asked.

A token of my love to the girl with a golden heart," said Kasthuri as she gently touched Suchi's cheek. Suchi opened the cover to find a beautiful, lemon-yellow Kanjeevaram saree with an equally lovely gold border. A touched Suchi lovingly embraced Kasthuri.

"And this is for you, *Kanna!*" Kasthuri said as she handed Krishna another cover. Krishna took a small box from the bag, containing a stylish HMT gentleman's watch with a large round dial. "Wow! This looks great, *Amma!* Thank you!" he said, trying it on right away.

"Malathi, my dear! This one is for you!" she said, handing Malathi a small red pouch. Malathi opened the pouch to find a pair of beautiful, glittery silver anklets. As Malathi looked up at Kasthuri in surprise, Kasthuri pulled her daughter-in-law into a tight embrace and said, "None of this would have been possible without your help and cooperation, my darling."

She then handed Abhijeet, Divya, and Vasu an envelope each containing cash. With an affectionate smile, she said, "You can buy clothes of your choice," much to the trio's delight.

"How I wish Vishu and Anu were here too!" Kasthuri missed her daughter and her family on this happy occasion. As she wiped an involuntary tear from her eye, she asked Krishna, "When will we receive the Certificate and the marks sheet?"

"In a month from now, *Amma!* The University will hold a small convocation ceremony where certificates will be presented," Krishna replied.

As they happily chatted, Kasthuri's friends, Akash, Aarti, and Prajakta, walked in with a beautiful bouquet for Kasthuri.

"*Aaji*, Congratulations! We are thrilled for you!" Aarti said. "And so very proud of you," Akash added.

Kasthuri affectionately pulled the three of them closer. "Congratulations to the three of you, too, for passing out with a distinction, and I'm equally proud of you, she said." The guests left after enjoying an elaborate South Indian lunch lovingly prepared by Malathi.

In the meantime, Krishna was determined to make the convocation ceremony a memorable and joyful day for his mother. When he spoke to Visala over the weekend, Krishna asked if she and her family could come to Bombay for Kasthuri's convocation, to which Visala excitedly agreed.

Krishna also invited Jagannath and Shashi, along with their families, to the convocation. He wished to ask his mother's older siblings, but they were too old to travel to Bombay. Therefore, he only invited Bhagwan, who had retired as an Army Colonel and stayed in Delhi. Krishna ensured that Kasthuri was unaware of what was transpiring.

Visala and her family were the first to arrive. Their flight landed in Bombay around midnight, and as it was very late by the time they reached home, they did not wake Kasthuri, who was blissfully asleep. Early the following day, when she walked into the living room, Kasthuri couldn't believe her eyes upon seeing Visala and her family sitting there, waiting to surprise her. She was pleasantly shocked and let out a happy shriek as she rushed toward them, overwhelmed with joy and disbelief. The other family members also began to arrive, and Kasthuri's happiness knew no bounds.

"This is the best gift you could have ever given me, Kanna!" Kasthuri said to Krishna, her eyes sparkling with love and affection for her son.

Amidst fun and frolic, the day everyone was waiting for finally arrived. Everyone was dressed in their finest clothes and ready to leave for the venue, a small indoor auditorium within the University. Kasthuri was the epitome of dignity and grace, dressed in a sky-blue *Kashmiri* silk saree that her brother, Bhagwan, had lovingly brought for her from Delhi. She styled her hair in a tight bun and wore a simple *Chandrahara* chain and a couple of gold bangles set with white stones. Kasthuri was ready to attend her convocation.

Chapter 26

The auditorium and the stage were beautifully adorned with lilies, roses, and marigolds for the occasion. The students and faculty were seated in the front rows, each receiving a customary black robe and hat to wear while going on stage to accept their certificates. The students' families were seated in the rows behind. After everyone had settled and the mic check was completed, the ceremony commenced with introducing the Chief Guest, the Dean, and other distinguished guests.

After brief speeches by the chief guest and others, a small cultural show featuring the traditional Maharashtrian *Lavani* and *Povada* dance followed. Everyone enjoyed the cultural show while relishing fresh green *chutney* sandwiches and tangy *Aamras*.

It was now time to award degrees to successful students. The students were called in alphabetical order according to their names. Aarti was the first to receive the degree, followed by Akash, amidst loud applause. According to the list, Kasthuri was fifth in line, and soon, as the name Smt. Kasthuri Srinivasa was announced. Kasthuri carefully walked up the stairs onto the stage while her friends, family, and teachers cheered and clapped for her.

"Introducing the University topper for the year 1973-74, Smt. Kasthuri Srinivasa. Smt. Kasthuri has also secured the highest marks in five of six papers, which is indeed a remarkable achievement," the programme conductor announced. Krishna, Visala, Suchi, Abhijeet, and the children went wild with happiness, clapping as hard as they could. Kasthuri was honoured by the chief guest and the Dean with a graduation certificate, separate medals for topping various subjects, and a gold medal for being the University topper that year. Bhagwan was reminded of the days at Hardwicke Mission School, where Sir Albert Victor would present his sister with a shield for her performance year after year.

Kasthuri graciously thanked the Dean and the Chief guest before walking down the stage towards her seat amidst applause, her heart filled with happiness and a sense of achievement. After the other students received their degrees, the H.O.D, Smt. Suhasini was invited to give the concluding speech.

Like every year, this year too, we have been fortunate to have students who have joined this course with a purpose and a goal, and we wish them all good luck. Each year, the students have graciously thanked us, the faculty, for inspiring them. This year, however, the faculty has been inspired by an extraordinary student and a wonderful human being, Smt. Kasthuri Srinivasa. Kasthuri Madam, as we, the faculty, addressed her, joined the course at sixty-five to pursue her dream of becoming a graduate. Her determination, dedication, sincerity, and enthusiasm throughout the course are praiseworthy. It's no wonder she has emerged as the topper this year. Madam Kasthuri! It has been a pleasure and an honour to know you, and you will continue to inspire us all, " she said as she concluded her speech.

The audience, including Krishna, Visala, and the other family members, rose to give Kasthuri a well-deserved standing ovation. The brother-sister duo did not realise that tears of joy and pride flowed down their faces as they continued to clap for their mother.

Professor Suhasini approached Kasthuri and held her hand, leading her onto the stage. The entire faculty honoured Kasthuri with a silk shawl and a beautiful bouquet. The auditorium once again resounded with roaring applause. An overwhelmed Kasthuri folded her hands respectfully and said, "Thank you!" before slowly walking down to her seat.

Soon, the program concluded with the national anthem playing, and it was time to disperse. Kasthuri's family rushed forward and surrounded Kasthuri happily. Kasthuri bid farewell to her friends and teachers before exiting the auditorium, holding her grandchildren's hands. Once home, everyone sat joyfully in the living room, fondly reminiscing about every moment of the ceremony. No one even thought about dinner as their hearts were full of joy and pride until Malathi served them plates of *hot upma*.

"I'm not hungry, dear! I think I'll just have a glass of milk," Kasthuri said. She gazed at her family gathered around her and added, "Today has been the happiest day of my life, and celebrating it with all of you, my beloved family, makes it even more special! I feel so satisfied and content."

An hour later, a tired and sleepy Kasthuri excused herself and retired to her room. The others continued their lively conversations until late at night. The following day, Malathi was the first to wake up. She was surprised that Kasthuri was still sleeping, as she had always been an early riser. The door to her room was partially closed. "*Athe* is probably tired," she thought as she tiptoed back into the kitchen to prepare breakfast. Meanwhile, the rest of the family woke up too and gathered in the living room for their morning coffee.

"Is *Amma* bathing?" Krishna asked Malathi as he savoured his morning dose of filter coffee.

"She is still sleeping. Must have gotten tired yesterday."

"Still sleeping! It sounds so unlike *Amma,*" Krishna remarked as he walked towards his mother's room while Malathi and the others followed him. When Krishna pushed the partially open door of his mother's room, they found her sleeping soundly on her bed.

Beside her on the bed rested her beloved father's photo frame, her graduation certificate, and the medals she had received the night before.

"*Amma!*" Krishna called. There was no response. Visala gently shook her mother and called, "*Amma.*" There was still no response. Bhagwan also tried to wake Kasthuri and realised that his sister's body felt cold. By now, Krishna had become worried and ran downstairs to call Dr. Sawant, who immediately came up with Krishna. He checked Kasthuri's pulse, heartbeat, and eyes, then looked up at Krishna and shook his head sideways, his expression one of helplessness.

"Sorry, Krishna, Kasthuri *Kaki* is no longer with us."

Kasthuri had passed away peacefully in her sleep.

"Our dead are never dead to us until we have forgotten them"

– George Eliot.